CONFLICT
OF
INTERE$T

CONFLICT

OF

INTERE$T

Tyress Cunningham

Conflict Of Intere$t

Copyright © 2021 by Tyress Cunningham

Published in the United States by Ahtrae Publishing LLC

Dallas, Texas 2021

www.therealearthagatlin.com

Cover Design Lamar "Sheer Genius" Hall

Editor Megan Joseph, Joseph Editorial Services

Print book ISBN 978-0-578-91372-8

E-book ISBN 978-0-578-35021-9

Library of Congress Cataloging-in-Publication Data

Name: Cunningham, Tyress, author

Title: Conflict of Intere$t/ Tyress Cunningham

Description: Dallas, Texas : Ahtrae Publishing, LLC, 2022

Identifiers: LCCN 2021925696

DEDICATION

My first dedication is to the hustle and the cold, dark, lonely nights I stood outside waiting on some crumbled up money.

This is for the ones who gave me the do's and don'ts in the streets as they told me to go in the other room, so I didn't see them get high.

This is for the millions of lost souls roaming the streets with gifting talents, needing redemption and one opportunity.

Most of all, this is for you who battle with yourself every day and no one else understands the real conflict of interest.

ACKNOWLEDGEMENTS

I want to acknowledge everyone, from the county jail to the joints, for staying on my door asking for more pages and giving me the motivation in a very dark time in my life. All y'all know who you are. We making this happen for real.

For all the gifted talents, the exceptional rappers who contributed to the book, shout out to y'all! From a cell to a bookshelf.

To my mom for sticking it out with me and being by my side mentally and physically by my hospital bed when the internal battle over my life was at play. Every time I opened my eyes you would tell me everything was going to be alright.

To my granny the late LaClede Cunningham, for planting the seed of writing to me, to my Aunt Dee for her actions on making me commit to publish this book and take it seriously.

I want to thank Cathay for reaching out and doing everything she did and more.

I want to thank my cuz Demond for reading a few pages and inspiring his mom to take a chance on me.

Eartha, I thank you for taking a big chance on a nobody that's working on his change for the better. Thank you for the opportunity.

Carry God in your heart because He's always carried you in His hand. He's always there, even when you turned your back and ran. When you were blind and in the darkness of times, He gave you sight and whispered in your ear, "Come to the light and everything will be alright."

-Author Unknown

PROLOGUE

Even at night it was possible to see the light. Like a famous track star, he ran for his life. They set him up real decent. Spanish Fly even had the double-crossing broad Luv-Luv in on the hit.

If it weren't for the thunder and bullets raining down all around him, this would have been a pleasant night.

Money always had a way of making things change, like dollars to cents, friends changed on one another, from friends to enemies, known in the streets it was homies to phonies.

Spanish Fly was squeezing the trigger letting all types of lead fly at Popcorn's kernel. Popcorn could hear the close shots and the loud sounds of bullets penetrating objects, tearing things up. His eyes weren't playing tricks on him, he could see the damage the bullets had caused. There were holes making a large appearance on parked cars in the streets. Bullet holes the size of quarters, and that was only upon entry. Popcorn hated to feel or see what the exit holes would exemplify.

All he heard was BOOM…BOOM…BOOM… as the gunshots continued like a marathon. The sound of sirens was heard playing in the background, like beautiful music being composed. But over the shots trying to bring forth his demise was the rapid heart beating in his chest. Still, he heard, BOOM… BOOM…BOOM. Those sirens didn't mean shit at all.

The gun had a mean recoil. Empty .50 caliber shell casings littered the pavement. Spanish Fly knew he better capitalize on this moment or forever hold his piece. BOOM…BOOM… BOOM the sirens were coming from everywhere now. BOOM… BOOM…BOOM.

"Fuck!" the marksman cursed.

It was too bad Spanish Fly had to cut the fireworks short. So, he took flight in his Nikes to get out of sight. The Desert Eagle had exhausted all its resources. The large weapon was still smoking in his left hand. Getting caught wasn't in the blueprints when Spanish Fly drew up the plan.

He could still see the red and blue lights approaching and he was gone with the wind, it was time to bring the gunplay to a disappointing conclusion.

The gunfire had ceased, but Popcorn wasn't deceased. He felt up and down his precious body looking at his hands for any blood to indicate whether he'd been struck by what his supposed to be friend had offered.

Popcorn's breathing was heavy, his blood raced through his veins as he sat on the ground next to someone's garage in the dark.

Popcorn had barely made it. It was only by the grace and mercy of the man chilling in the upper room that he was still alive, but he was sure that wasn't going to be the case for the others who took part in the elaborate scheme of taking his life for granted.

So, this is how all the bullshit begins. A fucked up story on how a friendship can end in a blink of an eye and somebody gotta die.

My name is Tyress, they call me Woodz, ya understand me. I'm the dude in the flick on the back of the book cover. Yeah, I know I'm breaking the rule or some shit by speaking directly to you, the reader. But I said fuck it. I wanted to chop it up with you personally ya dig so you know exactly who it is you fuckin' wit on some real shit. So, take yourself from there and come over here and imagine you and me sliding through the land and you being my right-hand man and you seeing first-hand what the real smoke's all about. Now c'mon and go with me as I narrate this foxy business from my point of view.

But like I was saying, as you can see it done went up around this joint. Aye, I want you to listen up good, if they get to shooting again you better do what I do and hit the floor or you might not be around to read books no more. Every man for himself and I ain't going back to jail if something happens to you. So, keep your mouth shut and your ears open. Now come on and let's see what the whole business is with these two *kats* Spanish Fly and Popcorn. We got to move before the cops get on location.

CHAPTER 1

Before the sun came on the scene the declaration of war was trending all over social media. Last night's pow-wow was going to bring a great divide in the land. Unlike the past, there was going to be nothing civil of this war. Like an earthquake, the aftershock definitely would make people tremble.

This was a ballers feud, clash of the titans no doubt. In the concrete jungle, none was safe. No man woman or child would be spared. The wrath of these two titans would be felt by everyone engaged in the battle. Sides would be chosen, by choice or by force. Dangerous days and restless nights were ahead.

There would be no retreat. The only withdrawal would be pistols from the waistline. No surrender, only bullets from pistol play. The only honorable defeat…death.

His blood boiled. There was anger in his eyes, revenge in his heart, betrayal was on his mind, and a pistol was in his lap. Popcorn, with a black assault rifle in the back seat that begged for a chance to disturb peace, guided the steering wheel of the charcoal black Camaro, sitting on blinding 26" rims, wrapped in rubber band tires rotating across the asphalt. Two competition size T1 15" Rockford Fosgate car subwoofers in the trunk were woofing as he slid past homes, shaking family portraits on the walls.

Shout out to all my phony people that sat in my face and volunteered them lies.

Y'all hurt my heart and yes, yeah I cried,
But on the inside,
No teary eye, I'm still here.
Yes here he lies,
And I don't got time to sit and hear these lies,
That's why they play y'all song and fast forward and when they hear mine
They rewind…

The artist Maso Real told facts over the track while Popcorn entered the projects. The loud music and deep bass made his trunk rumble, waking everybody up in their homes like an unwanted alarm clock. The only person it didn't seem to bother was the well-dressed nine-year-old kid named Small-Time.

Even though it was seven thirty in the a.m., Small-Time stayed on the grind with high quality commodities for purchase. Small-Time was a silky little merchant with a lot of corruption incorporated inside him. His smooth eyes watched the man with thick, wavy hair, dressed in all black from head to toe, and wearing the humongous gold chain with the customized medallion of the state he was from.

Popcorn exited the slick ride, leaving it running and the music blasting. Under no circumstances could it be mistaken whether or not he was bearing arms because the artillery's handle was very visible, even though the gun was tucked in the waistband of his pants, under his belt. The magazine carried the ammo Popcorn anticipated he'd use to get at the truth, and nothing but the truth, as he headed toward the young dude Small-Time.

"Yo' Small-Time, come here. Let me holla at you, homie." Popcorn approached the miniature salesman. "You seen Spanish Fly?"

Small-Time had already gotten word of the assassination attempt last night. He found himself in a vital predicament where only the truth would set him free.

"Yeah, last night before he went to the club. He came out here and got me together so I wouldn't run out of merch, then he got with that pretty chick Luv-Luv," Small-Time told Popcorn while at the same time watching his surroundings.

To Small-Time's surprise, he saw a screen door swing open and the person behind the door added to the shock value. It was the recently released from prison muscle bound stud. He ran out of his mother's crib, as if ready to break someone's neck.

"Aye man, it's too early in the morning for that shit! My mama still trying to sleep!" the big man yelled at Popcorn with a whole lot of aggression to add to his intimidating body language. He had the bright idea of addressing them like that with his shirt off, flexing.

They could clearly see every muscle had another attached to it. He wasn't bullshitting, and he looked as though he possessed the strength of forty well-abled men, so breaking a neck or two could very well be on the menu. Matter of fact, judging from how he behaved, it was the daily special.

Popcorn didn't seem fazed one way or the other about the man's bulky appearance. Popcorn looked upside the man's head, amused at the antics the man had displayed.

Small-Time, on the other hand, didn't have the same impression as Popcorn. He didn't see anything hilarious about this at all. Small-Time's facial expression was plastered with more concern about the situation than any other emotion. Small-Time's life had practically just begun, he was born healthy and strong and wanted to remain that way. Small-Time enjoyed chasing girls, running from police, and on occasion, bending down on one knee to shoot dice. So, he felt he was too young to become a quadriplegic.

Then, the convict pointed a finger at Small-Time.

"And you! You little mafucka! Didn't I just tell yo' little ass yesterday to stay da fuck from out in front of my mama's house selling that shit?" he reminded Small-Time about the zoning permits for that area. Instantly, Small-Time realized he didn't possess a peddler's license to sell there.

The muscle-bound stud was head strong, but little did he know he was jumping the gun. While he was addressing Small-Time, Popcorn's back was to him, so his vision was disturbed.

"Aye, my nigga, you act like you don't hea-…Ahhh!" said the convict.

Popcorn spun around fast with the pistol, anticipating meeting the mouth of the convict. Popcorn caught him right smack dab in the middle of his chops, knocking out his top and bottom fronts. Blood and teeth left the man's head, flying through the atmosphere until they introduced themselves to the concrete.

"Huh! Who you think you talking to?" Popcorn asked the man, while he reached back and slapped more teeth from his head with the gun. Now, it was becoming a family reunion on the concrete when his molars and wisdom teeth rejoined the tops and bottoms down there.

"Ahh!... C'mon man stop! Ahhh…Shit…Stop man! Ahhh!" the man begged for mercy, but Popcorn didn't understand the meaning.

"Huh… Shut the fuck up! Who the fuck you talkin' to, my nigga!" He continued swinging and asking his questions, trying to finish the new dental work.

"Who! Can't! Sell! What! Right! Here! Nigga!" He was pausing to enunciate each word upon impact.

The hard, devastating blows and easy questioning began to seem difficult for Small-Time to examine. He cringed with every tooth that flew from the convict's mouth. The grizzly sound of intense pain didn't make it any better. He'd never seen a man that physically scream high-pitched like a woman. And somehow, the slaps seemed to get louder.

"Bet yo' pussy ass watch who da fuck you talkin' to next

time!" Popcorn was foreseeing the man's future as he relentlessly swung the blood-spattered pistol across muscle man's mouth. "Huh! Won't you! Yeah, I know you will!"

Popcorn had become fatigued, but just as the old school group the Whispers said, *and the beat goes on.*

"Huh…Huh…You gone watch your mouth, my nigga?" he asked the now toothless man for the last time as he brought the life lesson to its bloody end.

Popcorn looked at the ground where kids had marked squares with chalk for hopscotch. Teeth and blood were scattered along the sidewalk. Popcorn turned his attention back to the man, whose mouth and face were now identical to his muscles, everything was on 'swole.

"Ohh…Ohh…" he moaned in pain.

Through all of the tormenting screams, loud music, and the repeated questioning, not one brave soul set foot outside their door to help the man, including his mother. She and everybody else in the projects saw and heard that ass whooping he was receiving. Yet, they knew this wasn't their business, so they minded their own because outside that door was some foxy-business.

"Aye, Small-Time, when you see Spanish Fly, tell 'em I been out here looking for 'em! How much money you got? Never mind, you just keep it and tell 'em I took it. Oh yeah, you work for me now," Popcorn declared.

Small-Time looked at the extra-large, overly grown man wincing in pain on the ground with the baby mouth and made a wise decision. "Cool, what you want me to do when I'm done?" he asked the new general who was commanding the land by brute force.

"Don't worry, do what you do until I come back and holla at you."

Popcorn gave him his first assignment, then he kicked the toothless man in the ass as hard as physically possible, as a reminder of how Popcorn felt.

"Pussy ass nigga," he muttered to himself as he walked back to the Camaro, lit a joint and turned up the volume a tad bit more to allow the lyrics to penetrate his soul.

Now it's time for me to clear my mind.

Smoking weed, out a bong, it's happy time.

Beat a grown ass nigga with my belt like a sah-dah-tay-tippy.

That's Pooty Tang do you get me now?

I'm too stand up for you to sit me down.

I'm on the run for ah attempt right now.

Any other beef is six feet down.

Popcorn smashed his foot on the gas pedal as the enormous chrome rims spun, smoking out the parking lot. Then, the Camaro fish tailed, leaving the projects sideways.

Small-Time definitely was a capitalist. Capitalism was the American way. It was and still is the foundation of America. He wasn't going to miss the chance to capitalize on the musclebound stud's fragile state. He reached in his pocket and whipped out his cell phone; this was sensitive material. People loved seeing things this graphic. Plus, he could use it to further embarrass the convict. Small-Time began recording the aftermath and narrating the gruesome account.

"And look y'all, look at all those teeth on the ground!" he stated, zooming in for a close up so his social media viewers could get some real clarity on the content he was talking 'bout.

"Aye, y'all that's his mama right there helping his big ass. Ha! Ha! Ha! Ha! Ha!" Small-Time put the camera on himself laughing at the critically wounded convict wobbling and falling down with blood leaking from his mouth. He was being helped by his nerve-wrecked and shook-up mother, who was trembling frantically. That's when someone walked up, getting all in the background, so he had to cut the explicit footage.

"Aye, hold on y'all. I gotta take care of this business," Small-Time said to the camera, as he ended the live feed.

"Yeah, yeah, what's up? What you want?" Small-Time asked his customer.

The commenting ceased and the camera stopped recording so he could commerce. Small-Time knew there was no need to incriminate himself. He also knew he'd never survive in a juvenile detention facility and in his mind, he had no intention of going that route. That's what Small-Time called a waste of time, and time was money.

CHAPTER 2

Spanish Fly tossed and turned in his sleep, his mind wasn't functioning properly. The pillow he rested on was drenched in sweat. His nightmare was real and on the contrary, was not a figment of his own imagination.

He seemed a bit dazed, his consciousness wouldn't let him draw out what he already had confirmation on. The worst thing he could've done in the world, was to go against himself, he'd lose every single time, hands down. But to crucifix his man, Popcorn, to go against him, was like looking in the mirror at himself, and to know, he had crossed himself. The reality was his days were numbered and coming to a devastating end.

The trigonometrical equations left him overwhelmed with anxiety. Spanish Fly had crossed the point of no return and a friend at the same time. He had created the problem and the only solution was the loss of a life.

But just like Spanish Fly, Luv Luv had put her brain power to work on the difficult mathematical equation, too. She had divided and added, trying to do some subtraction, but in the end, she still wound up not solving the probability. Luv Luv had replayed the encounter with Popcorn. During the encounter, the devised setup, she had put herself in all sorts of flexible positions, making sure he felt good and safe in her warm embrace. In her mind, there was no way Popcorn should have still been alive.

Ethnically, there had always been a certain stigma attached to her. It was something that she just couldn't change. What else but black magic could be responsible for the strikingly exotic beauty of the creole mademoiselle? Luv Luv maintained a slim figure. Her belly was tight, showing off her six sculptured abdominal muscles and the perfect two-carat princess cut diamond navel ring. Her arms were slender, her legs looked strong, and her butt seemed forever swollen. Her breasts were exhilarating and brought a lot of unwanted attention. Her breathtakingly beautiful face attracted most people's undivided attention. Luv Luv had been made all types of propositions in her lifetime, including several marriage proposals. A few big-time modeling agencies had offered her profitable contracts, but to no avail. She stood at the edge of the king size Egyptian style bed looking like a queen in her green elegant intimate garment. There Luv Luv stood, as she watched the restless man with her piercing green eyes. She ran her hand through her full, curly hair, exposing her sexy arched eyebrows. All the while she wished she could do something to put his mind at ease.

She left the luxurious master bedroom, and placed her pretty feet on the black mink rug. Luv Luv felt the softness soothe her through her sexy pedicured toes. On her way out the bathroom, she returned with a dry face towel so she could remove the perspiration that poured from Spanish Fly's forehead. She could hear him mumbling, it sounded like gibberish as he groaned and tossed while he turned over and over against the thick comforter. She laid the dry towel on his forehead.

"Bonjour," she spoke softly to bring him comfort but received a rude awakening in the mist of doing so. "Ahhh! Aahhh! It's me! It's me babe. Don't shoot!"

BOOM! The gun blast was deafening.

Out of natural reflex, she raised her hands and placed them over her ringing ears. That only meant one thing, she was still alive. Luv-Luv was now faced with a real dilemma. The gray gun smoke was slowly lingering past her exquisite face. She went from offering comfort to being confronted by something that looked as though it shot cannon balls.

Spanish Fly had unconsciously drawn down on her with the pistol. He kept it camouflaged in the many pillows that decorated the large, Egyptian style bed.

She didn't understand what just happened. Luv-Luv was virtually staring down the barrel of his smoking gun. She was looking at death face-to-face. Luv-Luv came to a crossroad in her young life. She'd never experienced fear on the scale of this magnitude. She could see her whole life underneath a magnifying glass. Out of everything she could possibly think of on the earth in that precious moment, she only thought of one simple thing. The one thing that people greatly took for granted. The brilliant thought could be summed up in a single word: tomorrow.

Luv-Luv had to poise herself, before speaking. "It's okay baby, it's okay. It is only me. Your Luv-Luv," she said, giving him a false smile. The green, glossy lipstick on her luscious lips looked dominating. He loosened his grip under the spell and lowered his weapon onto the lush bed. She carefully and slowly placed her soft hand on top of his hand, helping him to further release the cannon.

Once she was successful in doing so, Luv-Luv jumped up, silently rejoicing and praising her supreme creator for watching from a throne in the clouds. She exhaled deeply, glad, and truly blessed to be alive. She took a glimpse up to the heavens with her mesmerizing green eyes, then she spoke in French, "Gardez la foi." The heavens heard her and smiled down on Luv-Luv. She took it upon herself to climb back in the bed in a feline manner, purring as she snuggled up next to her delusional man. Wrapping her slender arms around him, she pulled Spanish Fly close to her. Luv-Luv could feel the fast pace of his heartbeat pounding exactly like hers.

"Je suis la, Je suis la. Here I am, here I am," she told him, gently wiping the cold sweat from his brow.

"How the fuck I miss that nigga!" Spanish Fly yelled in a violent outburst that shook the room and her.

Luv-Luv released him, looking scared and teary eyed just as when the cell phone on the dresser broke the uneasy silence. It rang and rang. She looked over at the phone and then back at him. Now wasn't the time for any outsiders to intervene on their moment. So, she quickly made her choice. Whoever was on the other end of that phone would have to wait. Luv-Luv went back to what she was doing and wrapped her arms around Spanish Fly again.

"C'mon babe, let's lay back down for a while." Then, she released him and unwrapped the unworthy lingerie off herself.

"Uhh, where she at?" Sweety grumbled.

She was a bedazzling damsel. Her current status read single but Sweety didn't mingle. She possessed a body shaped like an hourglass. Sweety's brassiere was fully loaded, but she was even more blessed below the belt. In Sweety's past, her lower half had been responsible for many men being brought up on charges, accused of reckless eyeballing by their insecure spouses. But according to Sweety, in all honesty, it wasn't her fault. If she were to tell the truth, she had to be a cross breed between a human being and a thoroughbred horse. Sweety had been a victim of some sick scientific experiment. That had to be the rationalization for her hips, thighs, and astronomical derriere; all of which had a great influence on the public, in some cases men as well as women. In the public opinion, Sweety had a very distinctive, yet attractive appearance that was unlike her innocent, impressionable smile that lured her participants in even more.

Sweety pressed send on her phone again and waited. Sweety wanted to know if what she was reading on social media really had any merits to it. The phone rang and rang, yet she still didn't get an answer.

"God help me! She needs to pick up the phone," Sweety said aloud as she put the phone back in her purse and then snatched out her keys.

She was praying the comments and all the other foxy business on social media were rubbish. Sweety couldn't see two close friends like Spanish Fly and Popcorn entertain the thought of leaving one or the other as a recollection. It just didn't make sense to her, nor was it feasible. The Popcorn and Spanish Fly that she knew weren't built that way. They weren't cut from a double handed cloth.

Over the years Sweety had known the duo, they'd seized the whole land. Spanish Fly and Popcorn laced every housing project, strip, or block with their will power. Back in the day, they eradicated any and everybody who wanted to overpower their ability. Together, they beheaded snakes in the grass, trapped, caught, skinned, and transformed any ferocious bear wandering along their neck of the woods into a rug for everyone to walk over. The fellas from the hood didn't screw around because they knew Spanish Fly and Popcorn were nuts. They appeared to never have had a problem picking up a hammer and nailing down any problem they'd seen fit to handle.

Sweety was about to unlock the door to open up Spanish Fly's and Popcorn's beauty supply store where she worked. She paused at the sound of loud and roaring music coming from what she knew to be Popcorn's black Camaro's dual exhaust pipe system. Like a bat out of hell, she could see the Camaro flying around the corner, as she looked out the showcase window. She knew right then and there that her prayers hadn't been answered.

I got so many niggas changing up on me,
It's like a bitch when they walk, they switching now.
I'm so sick of bullshitting 'round,
I might rob my mans if he don't kick me down.
Rob his ass at the top of the staircase,
Laugh in his face,

Then kick him down.

I swear to god I ain't shitting 'round.

The bass coming from the car made her and the store windows tremble. As soon as the door opened, Sweety could smell the marijuana reeking from his car. Abracadabra, alakazam and presto, like a magic show, he appeared. Popcorn emerged from the dark, thick smoke. The eyes in his head were bloodshot red. He no longer resembled a man, but something much darker and more sinister.

Sweety felt like she was in the presence of a demon. She wanted to present a smile, but the fear inside her would not allow it. However, her eyes quickly became aware of the dried-up blood that collaborated with his hands and gold chain.

"Umm, Popcorn, what's wrong?" she asked.

Sweety's body had the jitters. It felt as though she couldn't stop the involuntary trembling. Sweety was totally caught off guard and was unprepared for the early morning encounter with the devil. Her intuition kicked into high gear. Inwardly, she knew one thing for sure, she didn't want to be exiled from the earth. As difficult as it had been, Sweety finally managed to muster up the courage to produce her invincible and irresistible warm smile. In the background, the music was playing, it's bass still pounded turbulently from the trunk of the Camaro.

"Awe, Sweety everything cool. I was just sliding through, checking on the store and a few other thangs. Awe yeah, aye you seen ya girl Luv-Luv?"

Sweety could see clear and present danger right before her eyes from the last few words in his conversation. This wasn't a trick question. She knew she'd better answer him with common sense or she'd become the third set of DNA on his attire.

"Un, uh, nope. Popcorn, I ain't seen or heard from her this morning. I tried calling her, but she didn't answer the phone. You want me to call her again?" Sweety responded as she looked at him, praying his reply would be nay.

Popcorn chuckled. "You ain't talked to her this morning, huh? Naw, naw that's alright, but you know what? Aye, call Spanish for me. My phone's dead," Popcorn replied.

Sweety felt her stomach begin to cramp and turn up in knots. Popcorn was luring her in some shit she didn't want to partake in.

"Ha, ha, no, don't worry about it. I'll catch up with them later. You just gone ahead and open up the store," Popcorn said.

He spoke with skepticism. Popcorn couldn't really tell if she knew about the home going ceremony they tried to give him last night, but he wasn't going to put it past her though. Right now, all he could do was speculate. So for now, he held off placing her name on the endangered species list. Popcorn turned to walk off but came to a halt at a thought.

"Aye, Sweety, do you know you have a smile that would make the devil think twice about being nice?" Popcorn said.

He smiled and at the same time fiercely mean mugged her before he walked back to his ride. Outside, Popcorn opened the door and hopped into the car. Popcorn sat in the driver's seat. He peered from the car window as he continued to watch Sweety, as if to look through her, to make sure she wasn't participating in the art of deception. Then, he slammed the car door shut.

Sweety could see her reflection coming off the tinted windows of Popcorn's car. She could only imagine what Popcorn was thinking as he smashed his foot on the gas pedal. Sweety almost leaped out of her sandals when she heard the massive car engine revving up and the loud growling noise coming from the Camaro's dual exhaust pipe system, water dripping out of them. She took that as a divine sign to open up the beauty supply store just as she was told to. In the distance was the fading sound of the car, which left burnt rubber on the street. The black Camaro snatched off down the street jaggedly as crooked as the driver behind the steering wheel.

My life is precious,

And I'll kill you for it with Rasfusha bullets, the host of a show when you come through.
They tell you to sit on down.
Got some hollow heads that will make you dance,
I call 'em boogie bullets. Now get on down,
You don't know who you dealing with.
Call 411 get some info now.

Sweety thought she could hear the rumbling and pounding from the car fading out a few blocks away. Inside the store, she hurried around and slammed her purse and keys on the granite counter. She let out a deep sigh.

"Oh, shit what's really going on?" Sweety pulled her phone out the pink Louis Vuitton purse and nervously started dialing numbers.

"C'mon, c'mon answer the phone girl."

CHAPTER 3

Macvicious was a hardworking man. Twenty-four hours a day, tick tock around the clock, the buck did not stop. Like a period to certain people, his occupation was highly disfavored. Often, the folk and outsiders, who were against what he was doing, demonstrated their anger by calling the proper authorities on his so-called company.

Macvicious thought he was thriving at the moment. His business was the Pleasurable Performing Act, Inc. that was established in 2020, otherwise known as the P.P.A. Inc.

His employees loved him with a passion because Macvicious believed in their abilities and made sure all the coworkers communicated and stayed within their jurisdiction. In Macvicious' opinion, this way business ran accordingly and there wouldn't be friction. He lived by the rule as long as fair was fair, he'd never have to exercise his executive order to take a man down. Otherwise, unless someone was putting the company's future in jeopardy, then and only then, would Macvicious, without hesitation, execute a removal proceeding, which could potentially lead to a perpetrator's grand farewell.

Still, there was a side to Macvicious which was no different from many other dudes in the game. He used social media as a means to be connected with the happenings in the streets.

Macvicious sat his phone down to give himself a chance to

process what he was reading on social media.

"Now it's about to get real crazy out here with these two. Bodies finna start dropping everywhere," he said to himself.

Like everybody else who had watched social media, he knew things were about to get rough. Money and blood didn't mix, not one bit in that life. In that life, it was hard to make a dollar when there was paranoia lurking, which led to the fear of constantly having to dodge a bullet. Macvicious' blood pressure was rising, leading him to sweat profusely.

"Hell, everyone was going to suffer under these temperamental conditions," said Macvicious aloud, as he eased his way closer to the lit incense burning throughout the joint to soothe his nerves.

"Okay, okay, alright. By tonight, I gotta get my business in order. I don't need funny money, this ain't no joke. I need to get plenty of pretty pennies. I can't let my piggybank be empty," he said, lounging around a large, round, oak table that was being cleaned and polished by his pretty, petite, sandy-brown colored housemaid with long black hair and gray hypnotic eyes.

As the Persian housemaid went about her duties, she was being professional and acted as if she did not notice that Macvicious glanced at her booty. The beauty strategically swung her hair over her shoulder. Her small breasts hung while she wiped and leaned over the large, now sparkling, table. She purposely stood in his sight in her red heeled shoes. Macvicious could not help but notice she had nothing on except for what she came in the world in; she was booty butt ass naked. Her face and body was pleasing to Macvicious' naked eye. This was typical though, so he knew now was not the time to lose his focus. He shifted his mental state back to trying to put things in place. He again became displaced from his thoughts when his female accountant walked in, dropping a large sum of cash right on the glossy table in front of him. He picked it up with both hands and began to thumb through it, getting a ballpark figure of how much loot was dropped on him.

Macvicious knew in his mind that in some places he would be hung from the gallows for how he manifested and facilitated in the dark shadows behind the scenes. Although Macvicious was light in weight, he was still considered heavy in the game. He was known as the small fashionable handler. He sat down in the empty chair sitting at the table built in a wall. Alongside him was a shark infested fish tank.

"Yeah, okay this looks about right. Now we take flight. I want you to put this up, Anne. I'ma get with you in just a few minutes, a'ight?" He licked his lips and as he handed his hot and wet adulterating accountant the overnight financial accommodations, Macvicious' phone began to ring. He picked it up and answered the call.

"Hey, hey what do you do? I've been waiting to hear from you."

Macvicious was taking a very serious and sensitive call. He listened to what was being said with a keen ear. His eyes watched in admiration at the fascinating job his cleaning lady was doing. What Macvicious mostly admired was how she portrayed the image like she wasn't hustling.

"Mmmhmm, I hear you. Yeah, that sounds great. Magnificent," he said with a pleasing facial expression as he continued being a sponge, soaking up everything being spilled to him from the other end of the phone.

"Right, right yeah, yeah, okay."

He had time to take into account that in the corner of his eye, his accountant had exited the room only to reappear without her formal apparel on. Her clothing was detached from her voluptuous, promiscuous body. She'd let her hair lay comfortably on her shoulders.

Macvicious took in her sweet-smelling body oil that she'd rubbed all over herself, seemingly not missing one spot, from her head to her beautiful bare feet. Her expresso mixed with cream complexion blended to a glistening cappuccino glow.

"Yeah, I'm still listening," Macvicious said, continuing to carry on with his important conversation and reassuring the person on the other end of the phone that they had his full attention. He sat at the end of the table unfazed by the extremely smart and beautiful woman standing there totally naked, except for her reading glasses and wedding ring.

"Yeah, mmm-hmm. You sure can handle it," he spoke into the phone and at the same time held up his other hand, signaling for her to hold on.

He let the brain teaser stand there and yearn for him. She rubbed her hands over her soft, beautiful, big breasts. Lifting them to her mouth, she licked and nibbled on her own pretty nipples.

"Uh, mmm. Mmm," she quietly moaned, trying to respect the fact that Macvicious was on the phone. She was hot and ready to mole over a few numbers she found on the books that were unaccounted for with management.

The cleaning lady's beautiful eyes locked on him. Macvicious caught the eye contact and gave her a wink, giving her his consent. She dropped the dust rag, walked over, and dropped to her knees. She placed her hand between the accountant's thick thighs, moving gently around the woman's moist secretion.

"Unh," the accountant moaned, still nursing her own breast while the cleaning lady used her long, warm tongue to thump the accountant's clitoris, sending a tingling sensation of pleasure through the accountant's body.

"Whoo, oooh! Unh," she moaned, clinching the cleaning lady's head from behind. The pretty Persian lady moved her fingers in and out the hot spot, arousing the accountant even more with the gesture, making her begin to give in.

"Ooh. Please, please, wait! Unh, please!" The maid's tongue licked up and down. "No, no, please. Unh, wait… please."

It was too late. Standing there with her hands gripping the

back of the cleaning lady's head, her weak legs shook recklessly. The accountant pulled the cleaning lady's head back fast and she splashed uncontrollably. The cleaning lady's face and breast were dripping wet as she went back between the accountant's trembling legs.

"Alright, then. Well, make sure you let me know," Macvicious said, ending his informative conversation and taking notice of the sexual sensation taking place right before his face.

She wasn't through. This is what she did. The pretty Persian lady's tongue was still playing in pearl city.

"Ooh my god, mmm. Unh. What-what is happening?" the accountant moaned in surrender, breathing heavily. Her stomach was moving in and out with each deep breath. "Unh, ooh no-no-no, please!" she screamed out as her body was shivering all over. She quickly moved the maid's head back again and when she looked down, she could see her long, pink tongue lick her lips. The accountant squatted, then there was another sound of warm liquid splashing on the hardwood floor entertaining his ear.

"Now you know you gotta clean that up. Why you got her doing all that?" he reminded the cleaning lady, who went back to tongue kissing the accountant's warm, wet pleasure zone.

"Aah, mmm, ooh, ooh, god!"

He watched one beautiful woman squatting with warm juices running down her shaking legs, while the other beautiful woman's head was between her quivering thighs, her mouth full of sexual content.

"Please! Unh! Unh! Unh!"

"Aye, don't forget what I just said," he said one more time to remind the cleaning lady who kept her mouth full and shook her head in acknowledgment. She continued to make it rain in the house.

"Unh, unh, ooh, mmm huh," the accountant moaned, not being able to contain her emotions. By all that was going on, Macvicious was more than aroused with sexual desire. He wanted to grab an umbrella and go play in the rain, so to speak, but he knew he had to keep a level head for now and refrain from joining the two women in his home. He had more important business to attend to. So instead, Macvicious got up from the table and excused himself from the room. Macvicious walked past both ladies, making sure he didn't step in the large puddle of the adulterous accountant's uncontrollable body fluid.

Walking past, he saw how the accountant's eyes were rolling around in her head from satisfaction. Right then, Macvicious knew his cleaning lady was going to have much more to clean up. He placed his lips on the forehead of the sweaty accountant, then he kneeled down and pulled his pretty Persian cleaning lady by her long black hair, away from the accountant's pleasure zone and placed his lips on her sweaty forehead as juices dripped from her chin.

"I gotta take care of a few things, but I'm coming back in a minute," he whispered to them, then he put her face back where he got it from.

"Whoo! Unh, mmm."

Macvicious continued to ignore the groans as he walked out of the room, dialing numbers on his cell phone.

"Unh, uhm, please baby! Unh don't, goo… Unh," pleaded the accountant.

Macvicious heard his accountant beg for him to stay and play from the other room. He acted as if he hadn't heard a word of it as he put the phone to his ear. Simultaneously, he heard the ringing from the phone as well as the pleasure sounds permeating the air.

"Hello, what's up?" he began to conduct business.

Spanish Fly had just finished getting out of the H2O after making love to his woman. He stood in the doorway wearing a dry towel wrapped around his waist. He couldn't help but to take a moment to gaze upon his beautiful goddess. Half of her naked body was exposed, as she laid in bed with the covers partially draped across her body. Spanish Fly visualized Luv-Luv's attention seeking breasts and light skinned tone body appeared to say hi, wanting to play peekaboo with him. They had already played love games and Luv-Luv was the winner.

It was now time for him to take care of Popcorn like he planned on. He had to live with his choices. Spanish Fly was on cutthroat business. He had made the decision to cut ties with his childhood friend Popcorn over power, jealousy, and respect. There was no turning back now. How could he? Like his woman had mentioned to him earlier, he had money. There wasn't any need for friends and she had also informed him of the reckless eyeballing his friend Popcorn had done to her, making her feel uncomfortable.

He walked to the closet and began to select his clothes. He chose a white and light blue jacket to wear over a white T shirt, then he removed the plastic covering of his all-white, heavily starched, denim pants to put on over his black silk boxers. Then Spanish Fly chose a pair of suede Hush Puppy shoes to complete his look. *To stomp down* as he called it.

Spanish Fly replayed the events from last night over and over. He had missed a chance to take his ex-friend out, but as soon as the opportunity made itself available again, he was going to make damn sure Popcorn didn't survive their next encounter. After the first murder attempt, he'd made himself that promise.

"Damn, how could I have missed?" he asked himself while he checked himself out in the full-length mirror on the wall. "But when I catch 'yo ass again, I'ma blow 'yo ass out 'yo shoes, please trust and believe me."

As he continued to motivate himself to double cross his man's like a four-lane intersection.

"Bien-etre," murmured Luv Luv.

At that moment, he turned around to see his beautiful Creole goddess smiling at him, softly speaking to him in French as she let the covers fall from her body.

"What is you talkin' about, huh?" Spanish Fly asked her.

Still showing her illuminating smile, Luv-Luv pulled the covers up to conceal her large breasts.

"Oh, nothing baby. I wasn't saying anything serious. Where you 'finna go looking all good and shit?" she replied.

Spanish Fly thought it was cute as he watched her make a fake sad facial expression like it was really breaking her heart that he was about to depart. The sexual euphoria had vanished. It was back to the life and death issues they were now faced with.

"I'm finna go. I gotta go find this nigga and smoke his ass. This shit ain't for play, the streets for real. And plus on top of all that, I still got money to go get," he explained to Luv-Luv his new predicament. She pouted and poked her bottom lip out, making her look even more sexy to him and arousing his long-term goal. But little did he know, all that cute shit was about to change. To Spanish Fly's astonishment, Luv Luv became infuriated with his response. He saw the reaction in her posture, as she turned her face up and let him have it.

"Nope, I'm not staying here either if you're not going to stay with me. So, if you plan on leaving, I'm leaving too. I might as well go to work and get money, too, like you," Luv-Luv protested, hopping her naked self right out of bed.

"Look baby, lay back down and chill. You ain't finna be out there like that. Shit done changed. You ain't finna go no mothafuckin' where!" he yelled.

As if without a care to what Spanish Fly had said, Luv Luv walked to the closet so she could find something to wear. Even though he loved her, he hated the fact that she was stubborn, and it was an everyday struggle for him to keep from doing something abusive to her.

"Girl sit ya ass down some mothafuckin' where. You ain't leaving this house!" he yelled again across the room.

Luv-Luv didn't acknowledge one word Spanish Fly said. She continued to shuffle through her wardrobe in the closet. Luv-Luv acted as though the man wasn't even talking to her.

Then she stopped what she was doing to turn and look at him, rolled her green eyes in annoyance, and let out a deep breath.

"Spanish you can't stop me from going to make money. I'm finna go work, ain't nobody worried about Popcorn," Luv Luv said.

To show him that she meant what she said, Luv-Luv walked over and grabbed her purse from her nightstand.

"Who said you was worried? Did I say you was worried? Because I didn't hear myself say Luv-Luv was worried about Popcorn. Especially after last night," he told her, starting to get heated, but she had her own way of cooling him down. Luv-Luv reached in her purse and pulled out a pretty pink .380 handgun, held it in her hand, and placed the other hand upon her naked hip. Then she raised one eyebrow. She gave him a serious look, which led to Spanish Fly's immediate response.

"Where the fuck you get that from?" he asked astonished, but his imagination was running wild. He had fifty thoughts going through his mind, like, *if she had a pistol why didn't she bring it with her last night?* This new disclosure was mind blowing for him. Spanish Fly walked over to her.

"Let me see that," he said, holding out his hand. Her breasts were jiggling as she backed away from him.

"No! It's mine. See, look right here," she said to Spanish Fly as she refused to let him check the gun out for himself. Instead, Luv-Luv showed him that the gun had her name professionally engraved in the pink handle, inscribed with black lettering.

"Awe shit, ain't that a bitch! How tha… when tha?" Spanish was at a loss for words. He couldn't believe what he was seeing.

"What, Spanish? It's mine," she said defensively as if not needing her guy to give her permission to bear arms for her own protection.

He went from heated to boiling hot. "You know what? Fuck it! Take yo' mothafuckin' ass outside the door then!" he yelled at her, bursting out of the room, and seeing it was a lost cause.

Spanish Fly thought, *only if she knew Popcorn like he knew Popcorn, then she'd be overjoyed to stay at home where she'd be safer, 'cuz right now, it wasn't safe for her there either.* The Popcorn he knew was out in the streets right now on the prowl, searching high and low for both of them. Spanish Fly was far from a dummy, he also knew whenever and wherever Popcorn found Luv-Luv, he was gonna put a pistol in her mouth and make her suck on it until he blew the back of her head off.

Spanish Fly was now getting the distinctive feeling that Luv-Luv really didn't fully understand the inherent danger she was currently involved in. In all honesty, what was he going to do? The woman already had a false sense of pride by carrying her gun, so in his mind, the only thing he could do was make sure Popcorn didn't pop her before he got to Popcorn.

Luv-Luv heard the front door slam. He was going out the house and she was all alone. She shrugged her shoulders. "I can take care of myself," she spoke with total confidence in herself and the pink .380 customized pistol made specifically for her. Satisfied and holding her position, Luv-Luv went back and placed the handgun in her purse, then headed for the shower. She paused on the way there when she heard her cell phone ringing like crazy, but she ignored it and walked to the bathroom, turning on the hot water.

The steam from the scalding hot water instantly fogged up the mirrors in the bathroom. She put her pretty feet in the tub and stood under the showerhead, letting the hot water roll all over her body.

***

The move he had made on Popcorn the night before had Spanish Fly feeling like the weight of the world rested upon his shoulders. He reclined the seat in his snow-white Mercedes-Benz rolling on 24" single blade Chrome rims. It looked like a snowball sliding on icicles. Spanish Fly's chest was adorned by a large gold chain with an even larger crushed diamond medallion figurine in the shape of the state of Illinois, with a black diamond representing his hometown. As he drove in the white-on-white Mercedes, Spanish Fly looked heaven sent. He put fire to the dope and began to think on how his life came to this.

Spanish Fly inhaled the smoke. He coughed as he exhaled, blowing out the strong-smelling smoke, leaving the car cloudy. His mind filtered through the fog.

Spanish Fly was in no way confused about what he had done. He knew people had been waiting a long time and wanted the division between him and Popcorn, so they could get in the game. Spanish Fly knew those other opportunists wanted to get close so they could lay their crummy mitts on his and Popcorn's poker chips. In the streets, every day was a gamble. He heard how the homies rambled about him. The barbershop conversations got back to him all the time. The suckers and *lames* were always talking, trying to give a black eye to the game, period.

Spanish Fly continued to levitate, he would come out on top in the bands because at the end of the day, it was all about the money.

The cold hard facts were made with cold blood. He just put a jumpsuit on what he felt was unspoken between them. Spanish Fly wanted to spread his wings and do his own thing. Maybe Popcorn felt the need to plant his seeds in the soil. One thing Spanish Fly was most certain of was this, the land was no longer big enough to produce for both of them.

He always knew in the back of his mind one day Popcorn would eventually come to the same conclusion. Even though it broke his heart doing something he didn't wanna do. How do you find out if another man close to you has the urge to build up the nerve to take your place? The answer is easy. Put your woman in his face and see if he tries to open her thighs and get low and taste her surprise.

Luv-Luv was a lean cuisine, agreeing to go up on a silver platter to be served with room service in order to see if Popcorn wanted dinner in his bed, so it would be easier to put a bullet in his head. Instead, everything went the other way and here we are today.

"Fuck this, let me put this shit out and go ahead and go lay this nigga down," Spanish Fly said, putting the drugs out. He cocked the .50 Cal Desert Eagle. He was making sure that there would be no misunderstandings when he spotted Popcorn and started handing him lead. Spanish Fly pushed the ignition button to start the Mercedes Benz an Maso Real was talking in volume in his ear.

My bullets like the host of a show when you come through,
They tell you to sit on down.
Got some hollow heads that will make you dance,
I call him boogie bullets, now get on down.
***

Not only did the warm sunlight bring out the beautiful women, but it also brought out abundant business.

Tiger now had an occupation, and even if it didn't look good, he did what he had to do to survive.

When he wasn't working, he invested precious and valuable time in lacing his sons with genuine game. He didn't want them to pick up the hammer and nail somebody to death, nor did he want them to do as he had done when he was a young man running around with a hot head under the sun.

The truth is, he used to bathe and sin while sipping on gin and busting empty liquor bottles on the pavement in the projects. He was a wild animal that couldn't be handled and had to be caged from living in the bowels of hell to living confined in a cell. Then he was back on the bricks. Like the scattered glass on the pavement, he was putting back together the pieces of his shattered life.

Now with all that being revealed, back to the spill.

A curious potential customer cruised on the scene and let the window roll down with swindling endeavors in mind.

"Aye, Tiger what the numbers looking like?"

He looked over at the potential customer with their dirt bag antennas wiggling on top of their head. He continued to carefully use the high pressurized power washer to spray down the candy painted, broccoli green, 1979 Monte Carlo sitting on mirror chrome rims. Like presoaking vegetables, he was making preparation for the habit-forming hand wash.

"There it is right there in plain view." He pointed at the building, then he continued with his sales pitch. "It is what it is. Ain't no way around it. Everything I touch leaves here looking like showroom floor material. I wouldn't have it any other way and I know you got to be a person with high standards," Tiger said.

The potential customer glanced over and observed the extremely clean finished product shining under the sun with his red, beady eyes and a cloud of smoke escaping from his filthy car. Under the influence and still undecided, the potential customer needed a tad bit more encouragement.

"Hey mane. You want Macy or Gacy, sucker?" Tiger chimed in on the potential customer's impaired thoughts.

"Yeah, I'ma get it clean." He stops the '79 Monte Carlo he was working on to direct his new customer over to the waiting section.

"C'mon, c'mon, pull right over here." The mentally-ill, alcoholic, convict had flipped the script to get his proper chips. He converted his life of crime into putting a mean shine on automobiles.

Even though the car wash wasn't his, he was a dirty bag and they came to see about cleanliness. Everybody who was somebody came and spent a few dollars with him and the nobodies on their way to being somebody came, too. He was the people's choice. He stood tall and somewhat built. He had severe scarring across his face. It was only a reminder to him that he came from almost being put out of commission permanently due to a near fatal automobile accident.

Tiger stood in his work uniform that he was proud of and went back to spraying down the old school Monte Carlo.

CHAPTER 4

Everyday brought something new. Tiger saw the black Camaro ride down the street for the third time.

"Eh, mane, what's up?" Tiger asked the new customer who got out of his car and began to watch the Monte Carlo get washed up until it started flickering sunlight. He was coming to a full understanding why people came there to get their cars clean. The new customer was watching so hard that it took a minute for him to reply.

"You ain't heard? Spanish Fly tried to blow Popcorn's head off with that desert eagle last night, my nigga."

Tiger stopped wiping on the car and turned to his new customer. "Nah, I ain't heard and I still ain't heard, you feel me?" he told the new customer and went back to handling his business.

The car looked better and better as Tiger continued to wipe it down. The new customer could now start to see his own reflection in the Monte Carlo's paint job and everything else behind him.

"Damn Tiger, you really be cleaning these mothafuckas up, mane," the new customer said in admiration

"Thanks," Tiger said as he kept on wiping the car. Tiger wasn't the type to brag on his job. He liked to let his hard work speak on its own behalf.

"Awe shit." Tiger stopped working to see what made his new customer make a comment like that. He turned around to see the Snow-White Mercedes-Benz pulling up on the lot.

"Awe nah, that shit ain't about to go down up here." Tiger flagged down the Mercedes-Benz. "Oh, oh, oh, aye, aye."

Spanish Fly pulled up and rolled the window down.

I'm too stand up for you to sit me down I'm on the run for attempt right now and any other beef is 6ft down I know the definition of the word hollow but this here bullet ain't no empty round…

He turned down the volume to see how long it would be before he could get a well-groomed hand wash.

"Tiger how many cars you got?" Spanish Fly asked.

Tiger looked around and took a quick tally. "Hey, Mane, too many for you to be waiting. Make an appointment for tomorrow and I'ma get you in and out fast as lightening."

Spanish Fly saw all the other cars waiting to get touched on and came to his conclusion. "Aye, I'll be through here tomorrow no later than ten, have a spot available," he told Tiger and turned the music back up.

I got so many niggas changing up on me it like a bitch when they walk they switching now/I'm so sick of bullshitting 'round…

Spanish Fly pulled off slowly, looking at the clean and gleaming Monte Carlo Tiger went back to finishing up. Spanish Fly picked up his phone and made a call. He left out the car wash and drove onto the street and disappeared in traffic.

"Mane, I can't be having… look… look, see that's the shit right there. See what I'm talking about?" Tiger couldn't get the words out his mouth good before he and the new customer saw the black Camaro circling the block again for the fourth time, looking for some action.

Shout out to all my phony people that sit in my face and volunteer them lies y'all hurt my heart and yeah I cried but on the inside no teary eyes.

Popcorn had that song on repeat just like he had planned to repeatedly pull the trigger when he found who he was anxiously looking for.

"Yeah, it's gonna be some real smoke when those two bump heads my boy," the new customer said to Tiger.

The new customer made an accurate assumption as he watched Tiger put the finishing touches on the Monte Carlo. And just as promised, it looked like showroom floor material. Tiger wiped a few more times and was done.

"Walla, alright man. You next, pull your car up," Tiger told the new customer.

Still on edge from earlier and still no word from her friend and coworker, Sweety was moving along and handling the daily operation as usual. A few people had been in and out of the store. They had made a strong hundred dollars so far. The front entrance opened and instead of a customer Sweety became relieved when she saw Luv-Luv enter the store. She quickly switched gears when she remembered how frustrated she had been not knowing the whereabouts of her friend over the past few days.

"Where have you been! Oh my God! What's going on girl? You not gonna believe this. Popcorn came by the store this morning looking all crazy and covered in blood talking about have I seen or talked to you." Sweety looked worried as she spoke fifty words per second, breaking the Guinness Book of world records for the fastest questions ever.

She wasn't quite finished. "And why haven't you been answering the phone, bitch?" she said now exhausted from all the excitement.

Sweety had so many questions but received very few answers. Luv-Luv was acting like she had selective hearing. She only heard bits and pieces of what Sweety was saying and zoomed in to the parts of the conversation she wanted to hear. Luv-Luv was struck with a glimmer of hope as she heard the phrase covered in blood.

"He was covered in blood?" she asked, as her eyes grew large with surprise when she saw the puzzled look on Sweety's face. "Whoops," Luv-Luv gasped and covered her mouth with her hand. Luv Luv realized she had overreacted when Sweety told her he was covered in blood. Luv-Luv took into consideration that there was a good chance Popcorn had been hit last night from all the gunshots. She didn't intend to react letting it slip from her lips.

"What you mean whoops? What are you whispering for girl? I need to know something." Sweety had already been caught up in the mayhem. She didn't plan on being a sitting duck for too much longer period. Somebody, somewhere, was about to come clean as a bill of health on all the activity that had taken place so far.

"Okay, Sweety." Luv-Luv was about to fill Sweety in on what she felt she should know, but that was going to have to wait because a customer in her pajama pants, tennis shoes, and T shirt wearing a multicolored scarf approached the counter where they were.

"Excuse me. Can I get some help? I seen some hair over there I like." Sweety knowing she had been at the store all morning, looked at Luv-Luv to assist the customer.

"What you looking at? I got this Sweety. Come on girl, let's take a look." Luv-Luv followed the customer back to the hair section in the store. She smiled and endorsed other beauty supply products on their way to the area. Sweety watched as another person with two children entered the store.

"Hi," she greeted them with her warm and beautiful smile. All that changed the instant she felt the vibration on the counter and heard the familiar tune from earlier.

I'm so high you gotta climb and get me down, whip my dick and start pissing down. Ewww till you hear that trickling sound, pissing on all you bitches, who get a kick out of kicking a nigga when he down.

The unmistakable sound of Maso Real churned her stomach, and made her sensational smile vanish. There was no forgetting this morning. She didn't even wanna turn around to look out the vibrating windows of the store. The door swung open and Sweety had no other choice but to see who entered. At the store, she always maintained her professionalism no matter what situation she was in.

She turned around. "Hi." Sweety had made the acknowledgement with a shocking facial expression.

"What's good, Sweety? How's business?" She smiled, taken in by the heaven-sent aura Spanish Fly exuded all around him. He stood there dressed in all white with a glistening colossus Jesus head diamond medallion dangling from his neck.

"Business has been steady," she replied. Still in awe from his glow. She was gonna say something else, but another customer walked into the store. Once again, her professionalism kicked in.

"Hello," she greeted the young woman who seemed not to even hear a syllable because all her attention and energy was geared toward Spanish Fly. Sweety watched her watch him and bumped right into one of the shelves, not watching where she was going.

"Oh, I'm sorry," the young girl said, too embarrassed to even stop and pick up the stuff she knocked over. She just hurried to the aisle she was headed to.

"Steady, business looking alright from where I'm standing. Aye where is Luv-Luv?" he asked as he walked over and picked up the fallen items, placing them back in their respective places. Sweety pointed her finger, "She's over there."

Spanish Fly turned his head. Not only did he see where she was talking about, but he also saw how the eyes of all the women in the store were fixated on him. He acted as though he didn't notice them, while he made his way through the store. He turned the corner and heard the customer Luv-Luv was helping talk about how certain hair made her look.

"And that's why I never get that kind of hair," the customer paused at the sight of Spanish Fly. Luv-Luv wasn't impressed at all.

"So, you were saying girl." Luv-Luv was trying to get the customer to continue on with her conversation.

"You know what, I'll be back later, I can't believe I let time slip away from me," the customer said making excuses to leave. Then she put down the hair and got to scooting out the door.

"Argh. What? Why did you come here?" Luv-Luv spoke with frustration through her teeth. Spanish Fly frowned up and moved towards her.

"Listen don't be in here making no scene. It's not safe for you here," Spanish Fly whispered to her. Luv-Luv took a deep breath and rolled her eyes.

"Are you going home?" she said sarcastically out loud. That started to raise some eyebrows and turned all ears in their direction.

"Look babe this ain't that. You sitting here trying to play some kind of game, you better come the fuck on!" Spanish Fly said as he grabbed her by the arm, but she put up a resistance.

"I'm not going nowhere Spanish unless you going with me," Luv Luv said. Spanish Fly grabbed her by her arm again, and she pulled away from him again, but this time she fell against the shelf knocking it over, which got the attention of everybody in the store. Everyone, including Sweety, ran over to see what had happened.

CHAPTER 5

Popcorn was scalding hot; he'd been hitting corners all morning, like a buzzard flying in circles scavenging over a carcass waiting for the right moment to devour it. He endlessly circled blocks looking for a dead man walking. He wasn't quite sure this was it, but his red eyes zeroed in on a parked car still running.

"Oh," he said. His blood rushed through his veins from excitement. Even through the thick gray cloud of smoke a sense of satisfaction came over his face.

"But I'm still here yes here he lies, and I don't got time to sit in here"

He quickly turned down the volume and brought his car to a slow creep. Even if this was a coincidence, he didn't care, it was convenient. He pulled over to get himself together. He ran his hand that still was stained with blood from the dental work over his face in disbelief and exhaled deeply.

"Boi, boi, boi, anybody but you. Damn, man you have started this shit, my boi." He reached around and over the passenger seat to grab what he needed for his expedition. He was probably about to handle some real *foxy business*.

It was like a ritual to him. He checked and cocked the gun to make sure everything was everything. Then he hit his chest a few times. The reason for that could have been for one or two things, first, he could have been hitting his chest because his heart was hurting or second, he could have just been checking the bulletproof vest under his shirt and gold chain. Either way he opened the car door and hopped out toting the chrome and wood grain AK-47 assault rifle advertising death. Popcorn was gonna give every living soul where he was going a general education about fucking with him.

The altercation escalated. "Mothafucka you gonna push me?" Luv-Luv yelled up at Spanish Fly from the ground. The galvanizing onlookers gasped at what they saw and heard. Spanish Fly didn't look so heaven sent to them anymore.

"Oh no he didn't just put his hands on her," he could hear the one lady with the two kids say over his shoulder. That one comment was all it took to rally the small crowd of women. That's when Luv-Luv took it upon herself to play on the energy of the crowd.

"Ahh!" she screamed as she pulled herself up from the floor and went into attack mode. She began to swing her arms wildly catching Spanish Fly across the face a few good times. That's when Sweety intervened and got between the two, pulling Luv-Luv off of him.

"Girl? Girl, that's enough!" Sweety told her trying to calm her down.

Luv-Luv wasn't done by a long shot. She had bought along her purse when she went to help the girl who took off. It was laying on the floor from the fall she had.

"Luv-Luv what the fuck is wrong with you?" said Spanish Fly.

Luv-Luv cut him off. "Nigga what the fuck is wrong with you? Spanish I'm not about to go hide. Fuck that nigga Pop—"

His back was facing a door. Sweety and Luv-Luv's eyes grew large with shock and pure terror. Their chins dropped to the floor at what they saw behind him. Then the crowd began to slowly notice the presence of the danger they were all in.

"Awe, nah, Lord, nah! Ahhh!" one of the women screamed when she saw the man come through the door with the criminal intent to commit cold blooded murder.

"Bitch you wanna kill me, huh?" An illness came over Spanish Fly that very second. He became queasy. When he heard the first word come from the man's mouth. The person the voice belonged to made the hair on the back of his neck stand straight up and his legs kind of buckled.

Spanish Fly's past reappeared right before his eyes to a childhood moment when he hung around on the bridge. Springing through the drizzling rain in April the wild foot chase had kicked into high gear. The police looked worried as they scurried about, feeling put at a disadvantage. The perpetrator was quick on his feet and they had lost a juvenile delinquents' trail. Making a determined getaway attempt, the fourteen-year-old boy named Popcorn had left the police in a cloud of dust. If taking him into custody was on their mind then they needed to change their thought process because that wasn't gonna happen. No time soon, anyway.

He had shaken them pretty good. Now all he had to do was wait patiently and eventually they would lose interest. Being quick meant being out of breath. He quietly tried to fill his lungs with the moist air as he hid tucked away in the big bushes down by the river. The police swarmed the area but that wasn't what had his full attention. Popcorn could hear a frantic call for help in the distance. "Help me! Please somebody help me!" Between the sound of the police walkie talkies and them yelling at each other in their intense pursuit, Popcorn thought to himself, he was the one in dire need of some assistance now.

Honestly, how was he supposed to know at the time he decided to enter the small mom and pop breakfast diner to rob the joint there would be a brave honest police officer in the restroom relieving himself of decaffeinated coffee and bourbon on his lunch break? "Please help! I can't hold on no more! Help!"

Still hiding in a sweet spot in the thick bushes down by the river, "Fuck!" Popcorn quietly mumbled. He wasn't in any type of position to be lending someone a hand. He was trying to keep from getting caught red handed his damn self.

"Help! Please somebody help! I'm gonna die! I can't hold on much longer! Oh God please help me!" He had a hard choice to make. Popcorn didn't believe in help. Where they do that? If he got caught the justice system would sit him behind bars for a long time.

"Help!" Against his free will and his criminal conduct, he probably was going to lose his freedom behind this

"Fuck!" he whispered one more time before he made his move. Popcorn left the best hiding spot in the area.

"Help! Help!" as Popcorn ran towards the desperate cries for help, he couldn't believe the police couldn't hear it too.

"Where the fuck was they at when somebody really needed them?" he said to himself disgusted. "They got me doing they job," Popcorn continued to complain while still heading in the direction of the cries which led him to the bridge made of train tracks standing over the famous River of Life where he saw a boy that looked to be about the same age as he holding on to the ledge for dear life.

"What in the fuck?" Popcorn said in disbelief. They called the black water the river light because so many people chose to take their life by plunging into it. The drizzle had now turned to rain and there was a small rumble of thunder coming from the smoke gray clouds.

Popcorn crossed on to the bridge. He looked down through the tracks, moving very cautiously. He saw how the large black river ran with rage.

"Help me!" the boy had saw that someone was on the tracks, but he couldn't see who it was, not that it mattered. He was just thankful somebody heard him.

"Hurry up! I can't hold on. My arms are getting weak!"

Popcorn moved accordingly. He wasn't trying to be in the same predicament the boy was in.

"Try and hold on. Here I come," Popcorn told the boy as he climbed down onto one of the three pillars that held the bridge up. A flash of lightning streaked through the dark clouds, bringing the sharp, crackling sound followed by a pause. Then a violent outbreak of thunder shook the land.

"Aahhh! Shit," Popcorn cursed. He didn't sign up for this extra activity taking place. The rainfall was much heavier now and it seemed like the sky became angered at Popcorn for trying to help the boy. The clouds rumbled furiously over their heads. Popcorn moved closer and extended his arm out so the unlucky boy could grab onto his hand. The boy looks scared and unsure if he should let go.

"C'mon man grab my hand. You done all this screaming," Popcorn told the boy, trying to persuade him to latch on to the help he cried for.

"C'mon man I gotta go!" Popcorn yelled.

"Ah, okay," the boy said as he let go and held out one arm. Popcorn quickly snatched it and almost fell over the bridge. He was taken by surprise at how heavy the boy was.

"Eh, eh, shit!" Popcorn was straining and cursing, while at the same time trying to reel the boy in. Little did he know the boy's weight was the least of his problems.

"Hey! He's over here guys." That didn't sound good at all. Popcorn turned his head to look behind him.

"Hey you right there! Don't you fucking move boy!" Not only did Popcorn see what he didn't want to see, but all the guns pointed in his direction made it very difficult for him to try and save somebody's life, when his life was currently on the line.

"Oh, oh, whoa, whoa, wait, wait, I'm trying to hel—" Popcorn's pleas for patience was met with the clicking sound of a lot of guns getting ready to handle some foxy business. The flash of lightning lit up the sky putting on a fantastic light show. Popcorn couldn't concentrate on the boy hanging from his arms and the police pointing their pistols. The loud thunderous boom from the black clouds made his hands give way and the boy's hand slipped through his. He had lost his grip and the boy became a victim of gravity.

"Ahhh!" the boy's screams faded as he fell forty feet from Popcorn.

Pop-Pop-Pop-Pop-Pop.

"Ahhh what the fuck?" Popcorn yelled out watching hot lead sparking against the iron railroad tracks. Pop, pop, pop. The police were unloading without any further ado. Popcorn dove off the bridge like a gold medalist at the Summer Olympics. The police ran on to the bridge, only to witness splashes as Popcorn hit the water like the rest of the raindrops falling from the sky. Like the boy he was trying to save, Popcorn, too disappeared under the black rushing water.

One of the police officers looked at his coworkers. "He's not going to make it." He laughed. Pop, pop, pop, pop, pop, pop the black 9-millimeter service pistol seem to have a mind of his own as a coworker aimed directly into the water where Popcorn entered the river.

"Whoa, whoa what the hell are you doing?" the police officer yelled at his trigger-happy coworker, holding up both of his hands towards the excited man to cease fire.

He looked confused. "That was just in case he did make it," he explained his action. Then his face balled up with anger and he continued to say what was on his mind. "And what the hell are you yelling for? Shit! You were just back there shooting at him too so don't go yelling at me!" the coworker said pointing his index finger into the face of the other police officer. The police officer's facial expression looked as though the truth of what his coworker was saying began to resonate.

"Alright, guys calm down let's move out. We'll send a dive team as soon as the storm clears. Alright come on let's get a move

on goddamnit!" the police officer ordered the other soaking wet officers to disperse from the bridge.

After almost drowning Popcorn emerged out of the murky river headfirst with the boy clinging on for dear life in his clasp. Somehow Popcorn managed to find the strength and ability to stroke through the deadly current, continuing to strive towards the shallow water carrying the boy behind him. He could hear the boy gurgling water at the same time, frantically screaming, struggling to stay alive. Popcorn swam to a large tree laid halfway in the water and on the side of the riverbank. He pulled himself with one arm out of the water by a strong branch still dragging the boy along with him.

"Come on man!" Popcorn cried out. He didn't know how far downstream the current had pulled them but what he did know was that he no longer saw the police. Throughout all his heroic deeds, Popcorn, while catching his breath, noticed something glorious had come from this. He'd escaped the police and the hot shit they were trying to hit him with. It was unbelievable. It was a miracle. It was one of the best feelings ever and eluding cases so far. No one was going to believe this one when he told it. Not that he cared if they did or if they didn't, he knew how the story really went and that's all that mattered.

"Awe shit! No, no, no!" He remembered the money. The rain fall was letting up as the storm continued to move on about its way. His clothes drenched and sagged on him. Popcorn reached in his pocket, looking over at the boy whose life he had just saved. The boy was coughing and gagging and throwing up water trying to catch some oxygen.

"Hell yeah!" he yelled when his hand came out of his pocket with a wet wad of hard earned and well-deserved cash. He laughed sitting on the riverbank with a bankroll. The fallen boy laid in the thick mud on the side of the riverbank trying to control his breathing and his coughing. He rolled over to his belly looking up at the boy who saved his life as the boy was *quickly counting money.*

"Thank... you man..." he said between coughs, pushing himself up from the mud.

"Aye man did you hear me? I said thank you," he said again. Popcorn stopped counting his paper and paused looking at the boy with a still face and then stood up.

"I almost got locked up, fuckin' wit' you. Man, what the fuck was you doin' up there on that bridge? It don't even matter, I gotta get the fuck outta here right now." With a sense of urgency Popcorn stuffed the money back in his pocket.

"What's your name dude?" Popcorn asked the shivering boy. The boy stood up, so he and Popcorn stood eye to eye. His clothes, too, hung off him from being soaked under the conditions.

"My name is Javier," the boy replied. Popcorn put his hand back in his pocket to make sure his newly acquired fortune was well secured.

"Javier, huh, well they call me Popcorn," he told the boy. The boy was still breathing hard.

"Like I said, name is Javier, but everybody calls me Spanish." Popcorn laughed at the boy's nickname.

"Man, what's so funny?" Spanish asked him. Then Popcorn shook his head and waved the boy off.

"Nothing, nothing. It's cool." Popcorn told him as he continued to laugh.

"What is you laughing at?" Spanish asked him again. Popcorn waved him off for a second time. This time Spanish became angry at Popcorn's laughter and hand gestures.

"Man, what the fuck are you laughing at!?" Spanish said aggressively. Just like that, Popcorn stopped with the funny business and instantly balled his face and fist up at once.

"What the fuck you say? Uh what the fuck you say boy? Don't make me beat your ass and knock your eyes out your head. So, you can watch your mouth." Spanish stepped back with both

of his fists clenched.

"You heard me. What the fuck you laughing at?" he repeated himself holding up his dukes. Popcorn broke out into laughter all over again. Spanish's eyebrows raised on his face in confusion. He lowered his fist watching Popcorn almost laugh himself to death. This was supposed to be a boxing match not a comedy show. Then he saw the light, but it was entirely too late. Popcorn swung again completing the two-punch combination, lifting Spanish off his feet into the air and back into the mud from whence he came.

"I said watch yo mouth," Popcorn said once again as a reminder. Spanish laid stretched out in the mud stagnated. Popcorn walked over and stood over him. "The way you flying all over the place, they need to call you Spanish Fly. Aye I ain't got time for this shit right now." Popcorn stopped talking and looked around to check out his surroundings.

"I gotta get outta here before the police come. If you looking for me, I'm in the projects on Fate Street." Popcorn gave him a smirk and looked around again trying to take an account the best way to get out of Dodge. He made a quick decision and headed north back towards the woods.

CHAPTER 6

The sun took a rest, and the moon came out to finesse what was left of the night. Even in the dark it wasn't hard to see something didn't look right. Outside the lady's front door was now Ground Zero for all criminal activity being conducted in the Noware Housing Projects. The cursing and arguing could be heard right outside his bedroom window.

He lay condemned to a twin-size spring mattress bed afflicted with pain. He looked like a science project. His head was huge lying on the pillow and his jaw was freshly wired shut. The new taste of steel in his grill and drinking all his meals was gonna take some getting used to.

She stood in the doorway peering in the room on her battered son, thinking to herself where she went wrong. Only a mother's love would allow the woman to stand there. She tried her best not to cringe at the horrible sight of her convict son's swollen condition. She wanted to be sympathetic but the noise outside his window wouldn't allow her to. She understood nothing could undo what had happened.

Those little niggas outside her residence were there to stay for good. She walked in the room carrying a cup with a straw placed in it. She had crushed his pain medicine and his antibiotic pills up, then mixed them in his soda, so he could take them as prescribed.

"You should've left him damn people alone." A tear rolled down her cheek, but she continued to express how she felt about their new living situation.

"You only made our lives worse. Look at what they did to you and now you got them standing right in front of my home with all this shit!" she spoke with a great disheartening tone. There was nothing else she had to say as she walked over to the television and turned up the volume so she could hear the ten o'clock nightly news over the loud ruckus outside of their window.

"Our top story for tonight. Beauty and bullets. Earlier today a man walked into a beauty supply store and opened fire." The middle-aged news anchor could barely finish her story before the convict's mother walked out the room.

She already had enough bad news of her own. She just couldn't bear to hear anymore negativity. She went in her room and closed the door then grabbed her Bible off of the nightstand. She sat on the edge of her bed, opened the book, and began to read John Chapter fourteen verse one through four from the Bible. She knew only God was going to get her through these troubled days up ahead. The Devils playground was right at her front doorstep, and she could hear the demons outside at play.

"Ahhdee-Achaa! This is a stick up, don't nobody move but me." It had been the third time in one day that he had changed his clothes, but the results remained the same. He thought he was fresh to death as he searched all around collecting money off the dried blood stain ground. He wore a gray and black Pelle sweat suit that fit just right on his small frame and complimented it with a pair of gray Nike Air Max shoes that had the whole air bubble sole at the bottom of his feet to top off his outfit.

While he made power moves, the Cuban link gold chain, and the gold razor blade medallion he wore swung from his neck and glimmered in the night under the streetlights. For a kid as young as Small-Time, he came from where only a selected few knew what to do.

"Yeah, that's it," he said, feeling satisfied with the take. Small-Time was surrounded by a circle with all eyes on him. The gambling gods had shown him a lot of favoritism and his luck was as impeccable as his style of dress. He shook the white dice in his hand so everybody could hear them clicking in his mitts prior to shooting the dice across the concrete floor within the circle of anxious onlookers. His associates watched the dice roll on the ground. No one paid any attention to what was going on outside the circle which left them all vulnerable to what happened next.

"Uh oh! I see the shorties out here *getting to the money* my boi!" Bamboo announced as he crept up on the scene smiling and flashing his cash for all to see.

Just like the white dice rolling on the ground Bamboo received the same exact amount of attention. Every eye in the circle was focused on him. Bamboo was a true creep from the streets. He lied, cheated, stole, and committed battery with great bodily harm. Bamboo was with the shits. Whatever anybody else was on, he was on it too. The all-black shirt, dark jeans and black Air Force One's fit his character perfectly. Even the watch he had on his wrist was black with gold trim. He was in his late forties and the streets were all he had. He still looked young except for the gray in his hair had started to show.

"Yo, yo Small-Time, what y'all shooting? Twenty dollars say you don't hit your next roll," Bamboo said, trying to get in the circle to no avail. Small-Time picked up the dice again and got up from kneeling down on one knee. He looked at Bamboo from the inside of the circle. He stood shaking the dice, then he stopped.

"Aye, aye man, I don't mess with you, and you don't mess with me. We ain't from the same pedigree. Know what I'm talking about?" Small-Time enlightened him. Then he kneeled back on one knee and went back to shaking the dice. He rolled them on the concrete once more.

"Booyah! Give me the money. Bet back, bet back, y'all wanna bet back?" he asked his homies as he went to pick up the money on the ground, but he noticed there wasn't any response. They could care less about the dice game. The attention was still on Bamboo.

"Man is y'all gonna bet back?" Small-Time asked impatiently. Then everybody tried to go back as they were. Bamboo still didn't budge. He watched the little guy with hate and defiance in his eyes. It was the kind of feeling a man got when he had been shunned everywhere he went.

It was no secret that Bamboo had been black balled throughout the city streets. His time wasn't matching the crimes. Even if he was getting good time in the joint, he still shouldn't have been on the bricks. Some say his lips was loose. Some say he was working with the people of the State of Illinois. With everything that was being said about him it didn't dispute the fact the man would fuck over anyone and leave anybody for dead whenever he saw fit.

The truth be told, he had a get out of jail free card. He could do whatever he wanted out in the streets without any real repercussions. Then some said this and then some said that. But then some knew the discussions about him would lead to severe consequences if word ever got back to him.

"That's fucked up what happened with Popcorn and Spanish Fly at the store today. I never thought I'd see the day Popcorn shoot up his man's and shit like that," Bamboo spoke incredulously out loud while still playing with the money in his hand. The dice game came to a screeching halt.

Everybody stood up at the same time reaching and clutching their guns. Small-Time stepped from the circle still shuffling the dice in his clenched palm and a large lump sum of cash in the other one.

"Nah, nah, hold on y'all. Don't shoot em'. Man, them people

gonna throw us under the jail if we kill him right now. This nigga on duty now, he walking the beat out here talking about some shit he ain't got no business talking about. They'll give us all over ah hundred years for killing an undercover cop." Everybody paused, looking confused at Small-Time's new revelation.

Bamboo was from the streets, they'd seen him plenty of times in the hood, he was known for always being on some grimy shit. Bamboo thought he was going to take full advantage of the little homies but by the puzzled look on their faces, things weren't adding up as planned.

"Small-Time, what the fuck you trying to say, you little mothafucka? Who the fuck you callin' a cop? Lil' nigga you got me all the way fucked up! I'll beat yo' mothafuckin' ass out here for putting my name out there on some police shit," Bamboo barked ferociously, but his verbal retort was about to get him assassinated right where he stood.

Bamboo was questioning Small-Time's street intellect. That's when one of Small-Time's associates felt the need to up the Tech 9mm semi-automatic in the man's face. Small-Time's associates weren't going to keep tolerating any further disrespect from Bamboo. They didn't give a fuck if Bamboo was a confidential informant or not. Corrupt cops were found dead all the time round the way. They weren't going to just allow him to do as he pleased in their projects. He was either going to show a badge and identify himself around their parts or get smoked, it was as simple as that.

"Whoa, put that up. I got this," Small-Time said to his angry associates.

"What the fuck ya got nigga?" Bamboo said, unphased by the other boy who held the gun in his face. "Uh lil' nigga what you got?"

Small-Time started laughing, he put his money in his pocket and pulled out his cell phone.

"It's showtime! Aye y'all put the heat up, I'm about to go

live on the book." The angry audience looked at him like he was crazy, but they did as they were told. Small-Time pressed record on his cell phone and like a director, he focused the camera in Bamboo's direction. He made sure he got a close up shot of Bamboo's face, then Small-Time began narrating on his on the spot made-up documentary film he called *Exposure*.

"What'sup y'all, I'm back. I just wanted everybody to get a real good look at this face. Can you see him? Wait let me zoon in a little closer. Yeah, that's it. This mothafucka's tellin'! Ya' hear me? This what a snitch looks like."

All of Small-Time's associates burst out in laughter. Small-Time turned the camera around so his associates could be seen laughing and pointing at Bamboo in amusement. Then he put the camera back on his main topic, he noticed an unfamiliar face in the small crowd, one of his guys who wasn't in the last scene. At the time, Small-Time didn't give it much thought, he didn't think it was that important so he kept the camera rolling.

"This police ass nigga is out here in my projects trying to get me booked right now. Spanish Fly told me how you got old *skool* men life in the joint back in the day. Punk ass nigga."

Bamboo being accustomed to the old ways of the street didn't flinch at the guns being shoved in his face; he knew how to handle that part, but cameras, live action, and the new technology was a whole new element. Bamboo didn't know what to do. He was at a standstill. Small-Time was about to cut the camera off when he saw a masked man running into the scene behind Bamboo with an empty fifth of Hennessey bottle. Bamboo never seen it coming, but Small-Time did and he continued with his cell phone.

The masked man swung the bottle like a baseball bat in a homerun derby during All-Star weekend in the major leagues. From that moment on, Bamboo saw stars. He didn't fall right away, he stumbled forward towards the camera, his face in a daze. Small-Time was capturing some great angles of the assault with the deadly weapon.

"Aww!" Bamboo yelled from receiving the massive blow to the head. His legs were wobbling, he was trying to keep what little balance he had left. The associates along with Small- Time watched trying not to fall in laughter.

"Hit his ass again." One of Small-Time's associates requested like he was calling into the radio station and asking the DJ to play his favorite song again. The masked man didn't want to let his audience down, so he gave the people what they asked for.

So, without any further delay, he ran up on Bamboo and cranked another hit out of the park. There was a loud thud sound. The masked man perfectly connected the bottle to the back of his head. Every muscle in Bamboo's body seized up. He stood straight up, stiff as a tree. There were no moans or groans, there were no cries of pain at all. Like timber Bamboo fell to the ground. At that point, it was as if there was only one more thing left for the masked man to do. He stood over Bamboo and lifted his leg up and started stomping on Bamboo's head like a cadet in boot camp. The way the masked man was jumping up and down on Bamboo's head was like his leg was made from a pogo stick. While inside his mother's home, the muscle bound convict listened to all the commotion and laughter stemming from outside of his window as he helplessly laid in bed with a swollen head and wired shut mouth.

A chill ran through his body at the thought of what was happening outside. This seemed like a day that was never ending.

"You tellin'!" The masked man was yelling in a high-pitched tone and excitement as he continued to stomp down on the Bamboo's head with brutal force.

"Huh, you tellin'! Bitch ass nigga you tellin'!" The masked man relentlessly continued stomping on Bamboo's head and chanting. "Bitch you tellin'!"

CHAPTER 7

She said no, she said no please don't go, don't go,
that's when I had to let her know.
Born like this can't be faithful to no bitch,
I'ma P.L.A.Y.E.R I'ma P.L.A.Y.E.R you know what it is when you get off in my car.

I'ma P.L.A.Y.E.R I'ma P.L.A.Y.E.R you can tell can notice from afar.

I'ma P.L.A.Y.E.R I'ma P.L.A.Y.E.R,
It ain't no game baby girl I'll break yo heart.
I'ma P.L.A.Y.E.R I'm P.L.A.Y.E.R.

He was more than average, more savage than his cool appearance portrayed him to be. The only thing separated him from the cold world he was a part of, was the pure white wool coat on his back. No doubt it was the perfect disguise for the predator he really and truly was. In the field, Macvicious was a wolf in sheep's clothing.

The world looked much different from what he once knew it to be. Red and blue lights flashed outside his window into the housing projects where he once grew up and played as an innocent youth. The white and blue ambulance truck parked in the middle of the brick housing unit complex had drawn an audience of people who stood around dismayed as they watched the unfathomable. The paramedics were under extreme pressure holding the respirator over the man's face trying to revive him, while they multitasked and proceeded to hoist the severely beaten and unconscious man up on a gurney. His arms swayed effortlessly down to the side of the bed on wheels. The paramedics acted expeditiously because time was against them.

They struggled to keep the man's limber body on the bed as they rushed him into the back of the emergency vehicle. The paramedics seemed to use every trick known to medical science, as they attempted to save the middle-aged man's life. Macvicious sat comfortably and viewed everything while en route to his destination.

Judging from the way the man's arms hung off the gurney, Macvicious knew the man's journey would be short. It looked a little late for help. Whoever the man was, he was going to have to brace himself because nothing on earth could save him. Macvicious' car kept pushing and his eyes turned away from the window. He was very well seasoned; he knew that *foxy business* on the other side of the window happened for a reason and there was no reason for him to let that image marinate on his mind. He knew just as well as everyone else did, that what happened was only the aftermath of somebody getting out of line. With that thought in mind, he was still moving and grooving, the cell phone in his lap began to ring under the good music playing in the car.

It was back to business. It was back to the complexed game which he played with great enthusiasm. Macvicious answered the phone.

"Hello, hey, hey, relax for a moment." The stylish foreign Jaguar looked exotic, escorting him and three set of twins. The first set of twins were girls who were two college exchange students from Russia. They had changed their minds about college in exchange for becoming loyal students of the game. They mirrored each other perfectly. The two girls were identical in every way. The Russian sisters each possessed piercing beautiful bold gray eyes of which Macvicious was intrigued by.

They were strikingly appealing, if looks could kill, they would be charged with murder. Not many men stood a chance with these two. Not only did they have pretty and physically fit figures to die for but they were intellectually appealing. Unlike most Russian women with blonde hair, these two opted to wear their long hair dark, parted in the middle, pulled back and wrapped in an inconspicuous bun.

On this particular day's little money run, the identical Russian sisters carried a set of twins of their own, on their hips. They both were in possession of identical twin German Ruger 9mm semi-automatic pistols which made them the third set of twins occupying the black Jag. If anyone was bold enough to find out, who was who, the colors on their individual set of pistols could distinguish the two. One twin had a light set, the other twin carried a pair of dark pistols, purposely, Macvicious had made that the only way to tell the two Russian sisters apart. The final analysis would've been too late anyhow because by the time a perpetrator had tried to figure them out they saw to it that the perp was through and couldn't tell anyhow.

Macvicious tapped the twin to his right on the shoulder. "Hold on, turn that down for a hot second, I'm trying to take this call." He instructed. Both sisters sat opposite of each other in the Jaguar's cockpit of the spaceship. The sister on the left was called the pilot. She navigated the vessel with precision, while the sister on the left helped co-pilot every flight. She made sure the temperature and music levels were just right. As instructed, she leaned over and made the adjustment, bringing the car's sound system down to the appropriate volume for the moment.

"Yeah, I can hear you. What'sup? Talk to me and I'll talk back," Macvicious spoke into the phone. He listened intently, watching the deadly looks interchangeably shown from his twin assassins. They were stealing sneak peaks through the rearview mirror. The twins were trying to catch a reflection or any indication that some *foxy business* needed to be handled. They stayed ready to bring somebody to a dead end. Wherever the sisters went, they always were alert and very punctual, it was part of their job description. They never knew the time or place in advance where they had to go to work and purge someone who had displayed unrighteous behavior. It was just the nature of the beast, it was all part of the game, plain and simple.

"Yeah, okay be careful out here in these streets. And uh call me back when you get a chance. I'm about to pull up right now and make a move. Mmm-hmm. Yeah, you know it. You too." Macvicious ended the telephone conversation.

Right on cue the beautiful and immaculate pilot dimmed the headlights trying not to attract any attention as they journeyed into a dark alley. They slowly pulled through until, they reached a large black security entrance. Not far ahead, they appeared in back of a three-story brick old school structure with a small sign over the door of the establishment. As they got closer they could see the sign read, Pandora's Box, which happened to be the name of a gentlemen's place of leisure

The pilot parked right outside the door and waited. It was well off into the night. Macvicious looked at the slick Rolex on his wrist and like clockwork the black security door became ajar and out walked an employee with his *stray kat* tagging along.

"Mmm, now what the fuck is this?" Macvicious said, virtuously rolling down his back window when the phone in his lap began to ring again. So, he held up his index finger in an indication for his human feminine feline employee to give him one second, while he took the phone call.

"Hello? Wait, wait, what you say? Listen up." When he said listen up every ear in that alley became attentive. Macvicious began to put in the air what separated him from a square.

"Don't you ever call me again asking me what I'm doing, but since you wanna know, I gotta dame out in Maine collecting change. I gotta Idaho peeling a niggas potato back. My bitch in Wisconsin better be making a Milwaukee buck sellin' Milwaukee's best and last, but not least, I gotta chick out East in New York yanking wallets. Now stop wasting my time. You gonna compensate me for this frivolous call?" Then he pressed end on the touch screen of his phone and placed it back in his lap.

The *stray kat* murmured softly as she licked her lips with an appetite for Macvicious. She attempted to make eye contact but Macvicious wasn't having it.

"Who is this?" he asked his employee who had carelessly allowed the *stray kat* to follow her up to his car.

"She wants an application," the employee finally said. Macvicious stared directly into her eyes.

"Who said I was hiring?" he asked her. Immediately, his worker began to shiver as a quick chill ran through her body. "Mmmm, I wonder who?" he said as he continued to glare.

By her body language, he sensed she was uneasy and possibly shouldn't have been so presumptuous because she looked like she wanted to retreat.

Macvicious broke the ice and glanced beyond his employee's shoulder and had second thoughts, *maybe this stray kat had a promising career in her future*. He began to see some potential for her especially with his company. Macvicious thought he had a natural understanding for a person's desperation for what they would do to eat. So based on his own so called scientific fact, his belief was, feed 'em right and they came back.

"Uh okay let's make an appointment for her and we'll see what she can do on her interview, alright?" His employee smiled with relief and nodded her head for the kat to hurry away. The kat scurried back to the security door and scratched on it to get back into the building. The door opened and she eased through, rubbing against the security guard as the door closed back.

"Macvicious I—" he cut her off by putting his index finger up to her lips.

"Shhh. You can, with the right propaganda and proper grooming, domesticate a *stray kat* and put 'em on a path to cash." He looked back at his employee like she knew better and never to let this happen again. Then he put his finger down. The employee then proceeded to lean through the window to hand him an envelope. His deadly eyes met hers. Without hesitation, the Russian pistols were pulled and aimed at the employee's face. One gun was placed underneath the employee's chin and the second dark gun was precisely touching the soft spot of her temple on the side of her forehead, then Macvicious laid down some very important instructions to his careless employee.

"You better make sure that kat ain't a rat." Then he gave her a kiss on the lips. A tear ran down her face.

"Okay," she whispered. Macvicious gave his co-pilot a wink and the pistols disappeared as if into thin air. His employee stepped away and out of the window breathing heavily.

"You let me know what kind of mammal she is, and I mean fast. I'll be waiting on your call tonight," he said to her and then he rolled up the window. The Russian pilot put the car in gear and slowly pulled out the alley. The Russian co-pilot resumed her functions as well and like clockwork turned the volume up in the car, as they resorted to listen to the lyrics of the same song.

CHAPTER 8

"Mmm. No." She moaned in her sleep. Horrifying thoughts of her own memorial service haunted Luv-Luv in her dreams, all she kept seeing was Popcorn trying to kill her and Spanish Fly in the store earlier that day.

"Bitch, you wanna kill me, huh?!" Popcorn asked pulling the trigger and letting the chrome woodgrain A.K.-47 do the rest of the talking for him.

Faw-Faw-Faw-Faw.

At the first gun blast, Spanish Fly turned Luv-Luv's lie into the truth. He shoved her down to the floor. To get killed only took a split second.

Faw-Faw-Faw-Faw.

A second was all Spanish Fly had before his head would be fatally split open.

Faw-Faw.

The man nosedived out the line of fire, but that didn't seem to work. He was the primary target and wherever he went the loud gunfire followed. The tall wooden shelves fell all around him. Spanish Fly could see beauty cosmetics exploding over people taking cover in the aisles on the floor.

Faw-Faw-Faw.

The lethal force of the bullets flew everywhere, penetrating through the walls, ripping out chunks of drywall and concrete. The drywall was left with holes large enough to see clear through to the next room.

Faw-Faw-Faw.

Popcorn was nonpartisan, he didn't believe in discrimination. He was giving everyone in the store an equal opportunity to accept what he had to offer. Large hot, empty, smoking shell casings ejected from the assault rifle bouncing on the floor around his feet. The terrifying screams of innocent bystanders were drowned out by the foreclosure Popcorn was putting down on the now sanctified, holy building. Luv-Luv's eyes followed her ears now, from under the falling shelves and debris where she was positioned. She saw a mother positioned over her crying and scared children as a human shield.

"Oh Lord." She could barely speak because she found herself scared and crying too, like the two children being shielded by their mother.

Faw!

She couldn't help but to flinch every time she heard a gunshot.

Faw-Faw-Faw Faw Faw Faw Faw.

The gun shots kept exploding and sending louds sounds all over the place.

Faw Faw Faw.

Popcorn was trying to turn heads into pudding with what was coming out of the banana clip magazine curled under the assault rifle. This time he didn't aim to miss and wasn't monkeying around. He went ape shit.

Faw Faw Faw Faw-Faw Faw Faw.

"Ahhhh!" Luv-Luv screamed jumping up out her sleep like she had been frightened to death. She looked around the empty room and realized she was at home and not in a warzone. She sat in the Egyptian style bed wishing things would change. A genie would have to appear to grant her that wish. She now understood why Spanish Fly had tossed and turned in his sleep earlier that morning. Luv-Luv understood it quite well. It was clear as day that she was now on borrowed time, and she might not live to see too many more days. Things had also started to sink in that she and Spanish Fly had fucked up. They had messed with the wrong person.

They fucked with the wrong one and now the wrong one was coming back to fuck with them hard. She rolled out of bed wondering why she was alone. Luv-Luv sat back down on the plush bed. "Spanish!" she yelled to the top of her lungs. The bedroom door flung open and he appeared with his gun drawn.

"What's wrong babe?" he asked. Walking in the room and taking a seat next to her on the bed. He set the large black .50 Cal Desert Eagle pistol down by his side of the bed and held Luv-Luv in his arms.

"Shh, everything is gonna be alright. I'ma get that nigga," he assured and kissed her on the cheek. She came closer and laid her head on his shoulder.

"Spanish you got to get him." He rubbed his hand through her short curly hair. She lifted her head and looked at him. "Spanish, I didn't know he was going to get up and lock the door that night. I did like we planned. I got him to the room, he went in first and I walked in behind him and left the door unlocked. He went in the bathroom and before he came out, I was undressed. I didn't give him the chance to change his mind because he woulda left so I—"

Spanish tried to cut her off. He didn't want Luv-Luv to go into details about her and his friend fucking. He heard everything he needed to hear from outside the hotel door when he couldn't get in because the door was locked.

"Luv, I don't need to hear this. I just fucked up and now I gotta get him another way. Like you said before when I get him out the way shit'll be straight. Everybody thought I needed him. Who got the most money now? I do. I don't need that nigga.

Fuck that nigga. I'ma kill that nigga." Spanish Fly was on ten.

"Spanish you don't need Popcorn, you got me babe. You gotta get him," she said as she tongue kissed his neck. "You gotta get him," she repeated with another kiss on his jaw. "You gotta get him before he gets one of us," she said for a third time, adding a kiss to his ear to punctuate her point. She licked his ear lobe and then softly nibbled on it. Luv-Luv started blowing her warm breath in his inner ear and whispered,

"You gotta get him babe, Unh," she ended with a moan. She rubbed her hand across his stomach, then she continued with lustfully moaning. Spanish moved his pistol and removed his boxers. She was already half undressed when he entered the room. So, she didn't have much clothing to get rid of. He ran his hand between her thighs and discovered Luv-Luv was hot and wet.

She grabbed his joystick and began to play with it. Her hand moved up and down slowly. Spanish grabbed her by the neck and pushed her down on the bed. The foreplay was over, it was time for real business. Spanish opened and positioned himself between her legs.

She gasped, letting him know he was right where she felt him. She wrapped her arms around his neck and her legs around his waist. Unh, unh-unh she cried out has he went deeper with every stroke. "Spanish, ooh I love you," she confided in him while he was inside of her. He looked down at her beautiful face and breast and they bounced with every stroke. Methodically and strategically he laid down the pound game. She became wetter and wetter. Her cries of pleasure grew louder.

"Unh yes, yes Spanish, make me cum all over you babe." The more she talked nasty the harder he pounded. Luv-Luv grimaced from the pressure of him being so far in her stomach. She unwrapped her legs, but she still hung on to his neck. Spanish grabbed a hold of one of her legs and placed it on his shoulder. Her eyes grew wider, and she bit down on her bottom lip. He kept pounding her harder.

"Unh. Unh," her moans were getting stretched and coincided with her limp body. They were both caught up in each other's euphoria. Neither Luv Luv nor Spanish Fly was ready for the climax they were about to experience. Business was going to get handled on both sides.

Faw-Faw, Faw! Faw-Faw Faw, Faw! Faw-Faw, Faw!

"Ahhh! Ahhh! Ahhh!"

Luv-Luv's moans of pleasure turned to screams of terror. Popcorn stood outside Luv-Luv's house at 3:23 in the morning shooting up her home. Windows shattered and large bullet holes quickly appeared in the walls. A naked Spanish Fly dove to the floor snatching Luv-Luv down to the ground with him.

"Ahh! Ahh!" she was still screaming. Spanish Fly hurriedly found his gun and returned fire.

Faw-Faw, Faw!

He stopped shooting to see if he heard shots coming from outside.

"Ahhh! Ahhh! Ahhh!"

Spanish Fly was trying to hear if it was still on, but he couldn't because of his naked lady screaming.

"Shut the fuck up, I can't hear shit!"

Faw-Faw, Faw!

Luv-Luv flinched as Spanish Fly let off two more shots, trying to make sure no one was still outside. The fireworks were over. There was a dead silence in the house. Spanish Fly's gun was still smoking.

"C'mon, babe get up, we gotta get out of here now, the cops are coming." Spanish Fly stood up letting his nuts hang. Luv Luv was still traumatized.

"C'mon!" he yelled. He moved around the room to gather their clothes and shoes trying not to step on the broken glass on the floor from the bedroom windows being shot out. Luv-Luv had stopped screaming but she didn't move from the side of the bed. Spanish Fly grabbed her by the arm. "Come the fuck on Luv-Luv let's get outta here. Don't you hear that? That's the Mothafuckin' police coming, now c'mon," Spanish Fly ordered.

She took the clothes he handed her and quickly put them on, then grabbed some of her belongings and followed behind Spanish Fly. He took her hand and lead the way. He opened the front door, kind of peeked out with the gun in one hand and Luv-Luv holding the other. Spanish Fly and Luv Luv ran to his car, he opened the door for her and then closed it. He ran around the back of the car looking all around him and hurried up and jumped in the ride. The sounds of the police sirens were getting closer. He started the Mercedes and took off down the street in the opposite direction from the sirens.

Moving like an avalanche the white Mercedes Benz raced down the street at a high rate of speed reaching up to 100 miles per hour. Although they were regressing from the house quickly her time clock seemed to be moving slow, like sand in an hourglass. Luv-Luv's teary eyes gazed through the glass of the passenger window foreseeing the frightening truth.

"Spanish he's not going to stop, is he?" Spanish Fly did not reply. He kept his foot on the gas pedal, he peered back and forth at his rearview and side mirrors and continued to concentrate on the road. He felt like she already knew the answer to that question. Spanish Fly felt she was a smart girl, but he couldn't restrain himself any longer.

"This is what we talked about! This what you wanted. You thought it wasn't gonna be like this, huh? You thought it was gonna be easy huh? No power comes without struggle. Bitch you let the nigga lock the door! Bitch that shit wasn't supposed to go that far. He should be dead right now. You fucked up bitch and now this what it is. It's war out here. Until I get him, this what the fuck it is!!" He blew up like a car bomb on Luv-Luv.

His words had hurt, she had a shocked look written on her face. Heartbroken, his explosive comments severed Luv-Luv's soul, she was deeply hurt. She broke her stare from the window and laid her green eyes right on him.

She began speaking with a trembling voice, "No. No I didn't just let Popcorn put his dick in my mouth, I didn't let him beat my pussy to death, I did what I had to do for you Spanish, for us Spanish and now this is my fault, huh? Nigga I told you before I didn't know he was going to lock the door and what the fuck was yo' scary ass really doing nigga?! Huh? Why yo' punk ass didn't kick in the door when I was moaning loud as fuck? I know you heard me. Nigga you just let him fuck me and come all inside my stomach, while yo' ass stood outside and waited on him to finish. And on top of all that, nigga if you wasn't shaking and knew how to shoot right, his ass would be dead right now, huh?" She put up one hell of an argument as she defended her point of view.

Heated at what Luv-Luv said, Spanish Fly removed his hand from the steering wheel. He reached over and placed his hand around her neck and applied extreme pressure to her fragile throat.

"Dick in yo mouth bitch? For me huh? Nut in yo' stomach bitch, for me huh? I can't shoot right huh?" Spanish Fly had her neck so tight it looked like her head was about to pop off like a cork from a champagne bottle. "Bitch I ain't no hoe, don't you know I will kill you? I'll kill yo' mothafuckin' ass. You hear me girl? Bitch you better not fix your mouth to say no shit like that to me again ever in yo' life."

He was strangling her until she turned red, and her tearful eyes began to roll up in her head. Spanish Fly came to himself like he had made his point and Luv-Luv understood him, so he released his hand from around her red throat and placed it back on the steering wheel.

Luv-Luv was coughing furiously and deeply gasping for oxygen. In her mind at that point, nothing on earth was better than a breath of fresh air. To help her out Spanish Fly pressed the button to crack the window. The wind rushed in to give her a little relief, but it didn't help. Worry set in, when she looked at the dashboard and realized they were exceeding 110 miles per hour.

"Spanish slow down, slow down babe, I'm worried." Luv-Luv put in for a plea bargain. Spanish Fly wasn't in the mood to hear no sorry shit. This was the second time today Popcorn came for his ass. He knew how Popcorn played the game. It was time for him to turn up and turn Popcorn down. From that point Spanish Fly knew play time was over. He pressed the volume button on the steering wheel and kept putting pressure on the gas pedal flying through the night.

The big black kat was on the prowl and was camouflaged by night light. The black Jaguar moved through the province ready to pounce on its prey. Macvicious was out at play and had only allowed the new prospect one opportunity to stay. She had been very honest and open about her origin. He liked that she loved her native American heritage. She was proud to be a descendant of the Navajo people. He also like how beautiful she was, her light skinned complexion and her long dark hair went perfect together. Her body, tiny but curved in the right areas. What caught his attention the most was the way her luscious fragrance aroused his impulses.

Since his first introduction to her in the alley way, Macvicious' mind had thought about how her worth could be transcended across the universe. From the get go Macvicious was intrigued. He knew there would be plenty of charitable proceeds donated because of her. He became intoxicated by the new promise she bought to the future of his independently owned company.

When he got the call that she really was a kat and not a rat he let her come to bat for the home team. She had this night for training camp, if she could prove she could play the game and perform on a higher platform, then Macvicious was going to let her play in the major leagues. Maybe send her out to Cleveland for a night or two, to see what that do. The professional ball players wouldn't see her coming by a long shot. For him it was just a thought, his options were endless.

The Jaguar stopped as though it was waiting to see if its kitten was going to come back with a catch. His phone rang, but he declined to answer it. He sat relaxed in the back seat of the car with patience like a doctor. His phone began to ring again and for a second time he chose to decline the call. The door to the jewelry store came open and she walked out with and obese man planting a kiss on her precious cheek.

From where Macvicious was parked, he could see everything going on between the old Jewish jeweler and his new kat. The jeweler's legs looked very weak as he held himself up in the doorway. His chest was moving in and out quickly which only meant the old man was still trying to catch his breath from having a good time. Macvicious' could see the new employee wipe off the remaining sweat from the man's forehead as they were ending the treasure hunt. "You were amazing," he said.

"I'm glad I could help you find your lost treasure," she told him winking her sexy brown eyes while boosting the old man's ego before she soon left. Afterwards she composed herself, gathered her belongings and had cunningly slid in a few extra trinkets before the two shared a hug then as she walked out.

The old jeweler had a twinkle in his eye watching the girl twist her hips and sway her ass from left to right leaving him behind with a few dimes short. She turned to look back and just as she thought, there he stood, like he was mesmerized. He smiled, waved, and closed the door. She reached the black Jaguar and the back door opened.

"Come here little kitten, you look lost. Let's see if we can find you a home," Macvicious said, inviting her in to have a seat next to him in the car. She entered and sat right beside him like that's where she belonged, all along.

"I have a gift for you. I hope you like it," she spoke softly, bearing diamonds, rubies, and gems in three separate black pouches, on his lap. "And this is for you too," she said handing Macvicious roughly thirty thousand dollars in crisp one hundred-dollar bills. The car began to move with her in it. The new girl wanted confirmation on her job status.

"Am I hired?" she asked Macvicious as he pocketed his new worldly possessions and then he asked her a question of his own.

"Why should I hire you? I could just take this and put you back on the streets where you would have to claw for everything to eat." She looked out the window as the car was moving through the dark and lonely streets of where they were from. Then she looked back at him.

"If I may, I would like to give you an oral presentation on why I should be working for your company." She gave Macvicious a suggestion wanting him to know she had a good head on her shoulders.

"By all means go right ahead, that's what it's here for," he said, giving her permission to use his private property. She reached down and grabbed his genital microphone and put her brain power to work. She began the second half of the interview, trying to secure her a position in his thriving corporation. It was a private session, so the Russian co-pilot gave them their privacy as they rolled along, turning up the volume of the radio.

I already know what it is she wants from me, she wants love like misery wants company, wants me by her side, she say she sees the us in it, but I'm a Player she don't know who she fucking with.

CHAPTER 9

It was time to chill, and all was still. The night had ceased, and the sun arose from the east offering a little piece of peace. Fear was officially here, and the gun smoke was just now beginning to clear away. The morning light intruding through mini blind curtains and nailed up bed sheets covering windows, had the groggy people still with the yellow crust in the corner of their eyes on their cell phones tweeting like the birds outside. The earth continued to revolve in a 360 and only one person from last night was about to be permanently laid to rest in their final resting place.

The fearful people of the community felt unsafe and like hostages in their own domain. They were exhausted from having to immediately dive on the floor every time they heard multiple gun shots ringing through the night, and stray bullets coming from out of nowhere to visit their homes. This kind of violence wasn't new to the police department.

The police officers were sleepy and exhausted from their janitorial duties of sweeping up empty shell casings off the streets all night long and giving meaningless interviews to news reporters. The boys in blue knew what was up. They had spent plenty of man hours on crime scenes like this numerous times before. The clues left behind, over the land were none other than the infamous trademark of Popcorn and Spanish Fly's hot tempers.

Ten toes down and his ear to the streets, Popcorn listened to what they had to say along with viewing the news the next morning. The news was broadcasting about a shot-up beauty supply store and someone's home, looking like a warzone in Iraq and shell-shocked people looking over their shoulders trying their best to recant what they saw, as they peeked out the window for a chance to be on T.V. in an interview.

Seville knew Popcorn was burning hot and was going to have to calm down soon and cool off. Seville was up in age, but his mind was as fast as lightning. His hair had grayed with wisdom, with a body left with permanent scars from misinterpreting the truth. He dressed sharp as a whip and *was* slick at the lips. His mental cup was filled to the brim with life's gems.

Most of what Popcorn knew about life came from Seville. In his prime he found a way to make a quick dime from crime by catering to people's most inner personal needs. He was a master manipulator playing on the instinctive human behavior for pleasure, acceptance, lust, desire, power, and addiction and those that were cursed with the infliction of greed. He went by the name of Seville and calling him anything else would get you killed. He was the man Popcorn knew as his uncle. He had thrived and survived, the era of Bino, Scat, Sly, Slick and Wicked when *foxy business* was the only order of business in that time.

Seville no longer indulged in the game, he had retired and had become an ordinary civilian. Even though old habits for him, were hard to break. Seville moved about the den like a cold-blooded reptilian. He stepped through the double sliding doors of his living room wearing poisonous viper skinned boots with the matching belt. He had made sure the small caliber chrome pistol with the black pearl handle positioned on his hip didn't slip off his waist. The black wife beater t shirt tucked in his black linen pants accentuated the pocket rocket he carried.

Seville took a pack of menthol cigarettes out of his pocket, opened, then retrieved one of the squares out of the pack. Standing by the doorway, he lit the cigarette watching his nephew laid out on his couch in a deep sleep. Seville grinned as he let out the cigarette smoke.

Popcorn's gun laid on the floor trying to cool off and get some rest too. Popcorn sleeping with his gun at his side didn't bother his uncle at all. Self-preservation ruled overall, it was the first cardinal rule in the book of life. No matter how you looked at it, the game was over if he was slipping. Seville took another drag off the cigarette and the cherry at the tip of the cigarette quickly lit up the shaded living room. He walked over and proceeded to take a load off his feet and have a seat on the black love seat next to the couch where Popcorn was asleep.

Seville dumped the ashes from the cigarette into a glass ashtray sitting on the table in front of him, then released the thick gray smoke from his lungs through his nose, hit the cigarette and blew out the smoke. Not a nephew, but a son, Popcorn was his creation.

Seville continued to smoke the cigarette as his mind unwound on what was going on with his nephew. Seville played the whole field. He never was the one for having a family if his own. The life he had led kept him on the go. It seemed like centuries ago, since he was full fledge in the streets, but he remembered this part very well. This was the small print on the contract nobody cared to read. When they were signing their life in blood on the dotted line. To fully take part in participating in the deadly game of the streets. He knew better than anyone else, the company you kept was most likely to do you harm. The smiles on their face would deceive you as you got erased. Seville wasn't exempt from the rules.

He didn't get to where he was at in life without any deductions. Seville's taste for success was cut short in his life. Situations, somewhat, like his nephew Popcorn, where Seville had been tripled crossed in a lucrative business deal, that he'd brokered which left him with his tongue being seized. He wasn't a religious man, but he was grateful to still be alive. He would rather forfeit his tongue than forfeit his life. Even though he couldn't talk, his presence was always felt one way or another. He put the cigarette out and picked up a pen and piece of paper off the table in front of him and begin to write.

On the outside looking in, you would never find the truth. The streets were a good source of information, but how word travel, by time it got to you, the product wasn't pure, it would be stepped on, hit with the mix. That's how things got twisted all the time and somebody end up dead, over people putting the mix on what was really said. The news was no better, they always showed up on the ass end of things. Having the news reporters standing in front of a crime scene misinterpreting the truth to the people of the public. Guessing on what took place, trying to find people to put in front of the camera so they could fill in parts of the story.

Seville wasn't a man to beat around the bush to find out what he wanted to know. He was the type of man that would leave you battered and beaten and left for dead laying around a bush. If he didn't find out what he wanted to know, the noise from him striving his silver Zippo lighter to light another cigarette got the attention of his restless nephew who was turning over on the couch.

"Seville how long you been there?" Seville continued to smoke his cigarette and sat up on the love seat. He dumped his ashes in the ashtray and pointed at the note laying on the table he had written just a moment before Popcorn awakened and sat back on the love seat. Popcorn didn't sit up, he stayed laying on the couch. He reached his arm over to the table and picked up the piece of paper off the table and read it. That's when he felt the need to sit up on the couch. Popcorn looked at the note again and when he was done, his eyes left the piece of paper to see his uncle's concerned stare.

"Listen, give me one of them squares," he said with his shoulders hunched and head hung low. Seville reached in his pocket and gave him what he requested. Popcorn put the cigarette between his lips and lit it. He let out the smoke and then he let out a deep sigh of hurt.

"So, you wanna know what's going on? My friend and his bitch set me up to kill me. That's what the fuck is going on, Seville." Seville sat up once more and took out a piece of paper and ink pen and then began jotting down some serious shit from what Popcorn was seeing as he inhaled the cigarette smoke.

Seville had finished writing and slammed the piece of paper down on the table making a thunderous sound. Popcorn lifted his head at the rumble and looked at his angered uncle before picking up the not. He took the not off the table and it read, "What mothafuckin' friends nephew? I told you a long time ago about him when you first brough him around when you was a kid. What did I tell you once before about friends? I told you ain't no such thang. We have no friend's nephew; the streets won't allow you to have friends nephew. Sooner or later, they'll turn on you. Remember, I told you that?"

Popcorn finished reading the piece of paper and let out a deep sigh again, "But I saved his life," Popcorn spoke with disbelief. Seville shook his head up and down in agreement with his nephew and began to write again.

Popcorn knew whatever his uncle was jotting down, was out of love and to protect him no matter what was on the paper. Seville was done writing once more, but before sliding Popcorn the note, he gathered the other two pieces of paper he wrote on and took his lighter out and set them on flames in the ash tray. Then he put the note on the table for Popcorn to pick up and read. Popcorn grabbed the paper off the table and laid eyes on it and the note read.

"Yeah, you saved his life and for what? So, he could get close to you, so he could take yours. Like I told you before, you shoulda let the mothafucka drown, but since you didn't, this is what happens. Nephew, Spanish Fly owes you his life and now the time has come for you to collect on that debt. Now tell me exactly what went down."

Popcorn looked at his uncle and crumbled up the note and laid it in the ash tray and set fire to it himself. Him and his uncle sat there quietly watching the paper being engulfed in flames until it was no more. Then he began to tell his uncle how everything went down, play by play.

"A'ight check this out. This nigga's bitch called me at three o'clock in the morning and um she's crying on the phone, see what I'm saying? Talking about, 'Meet me at the room,' and I say, 'Meet you at the room for what?' Then she get ta talking about callin' the police and shit on my boi Spanish. So, I'm like nah you better not do no shit like dat."

Popcorn had to pause so he could hit the cigarette he was holding. He put the cigarette to his lips, inhaled deeply and held the smoke for a second. Then Popcorn released the smoke and continued spitting the cold-hearted facts.

"I'm tellin' you Seville, when I got to the room, I didn't see no tears and she didn't want to do no talkin' Unc. Just like that, her clothes started falling off her to the floor."

CHAPTER 10

Yesterday was a day like none other. Her job was over but at least her life wasn't. The police had drilled her with nonstop questioning about the shooting suspect that she couldn't identify. She knew the way the beauty supply store looked after Popcorn left. She had lost her job but talking to the police and telling them what happened and who was doing what would have had her with a loss of breath.

In her condominium on the twentieth floor in a high rise downtown, Sweety was feeling depressed and still shook up. She busied herself trying to do three things at once, her eyes were fixated off and on the 32" flat screen TV installed in the wall of the kitchen, scrolling through her cell phone reading people's reaction to what had happened over the last forty-eight hours, and she tried to whip up breakfast. As she was attempting all those things, Sweety's concentration was broken. She'd been startled and almost spilled her meal off the stove from the loud pounding at her door. "Oh, no-no-no. Not the police again. They gonna get me killed."

The source of the burning sensation in his and her eyes were coming from the sunlight fulling shining down upon them. After a night of blaming who was wrong and paranoia, they were feeling like the premonition in their dreams, seemed like it was going to come true. Spanish Fly had been moving so fast he never touched the brakes, he needed to slow down. Sliding through the streets, he felt the heat. They were riding in the snow-white Mercedes. Them and the Benz were coming close to a meltdown. It was time to lay low and they had no other place to go.

"Ow! Spanish that hurts, you don't have to pull me like this. I'm gonna do it babe."

"Like you did Popcorn? Shut tha fuck up and c'mon and do what the fuck I told ya," Spanish Fly said with aggression. Luv-Luv's pretty face scrunched with anger as she followed him down the hallway. The love games were over, Spanish Fly was tired of playing with her. The hairs on his neck was standing up because he could feel the breath of death breathing down his back.

He was under the impression that Luv-Luv was the reason he'd almost gotten killed twice. She definitely was the reason behind the set up gone wrong. She did what he told her to, the time seem to a halt. This was it, as they waited. Spanish Fly stood on the side of Luv-Luv with his hand on his gun inside the light whit jacket he had on. Luv-Luv was on front street. That's how the door was opened.

"Awe! Damn girl I thought you was the police," Sweety said with a sigh of relief. She turned around and began walking back in the kitchen where the news was still on. Luv-Luv walked in and so did Spanish Fly, right behind her.

"Girl the store and yo house been on the news all morning. I can't believe Popcorn did that to you, what you got to do with what's going on between him and Spanish Fly."

Sweety was talking a mile a minute and before she recognized the extra company she had in her home. Sweety's private show was being promoted without her verbal or written consent. Spanish Fly had to have been a fool not to sneak a peek at her huge bare thighs and luscious booty cheeks, neither of which were able to hide under the short tight white V-neck t shirt she wore. Sweety hadn't noticed Spanish Fly in the room yet because her back was to them as she talked and cooked over the stove. Even Luv-Luv noticed Sweety's sugar dumplings so she suddenly spun her head around to see if Spanish Fly was enjoying watching her friend's half naked body jiggle as she stirred the delicious smelling food.

"What da fuck is you looking at me for?" He looked at her and said and then closed the door. Sweety turned around with a shocked look on her face. Her breasts were large, and the small T-shirt struggled trying to keep them concealed. Spanish Fly couldn't fake like he wasn't taking in the view of her nipples bulging from under the fabric.

"Luv-Luv why didn't you say he was with you? Shit!" Sweety was mad, trying to hurry out of the kitchen. She didn't care if she burned the breakfast or not. She turned around to head back towards her bedroom. The arch in the small of her back made her ass look so perfect, and with every second it was meeting Spanish Fly's approval because he was quickly becoming aroused with an erection his pants. Sweety closed the door to her bedroom so she could change into something more appropriate.

"Sweety we need to get some sleep; can we stay here for a while girl?" Luv-Luv asked speaking to her through the bedroom door.

"From where I'm standing this food looks done," Spanish Fly said and walked around the kitchen to cut the stove off. He went and had a seat at her small kitchen table designed for two. That's when he saw what he'd been seeing all night on T.V. He watched as the news reporter stood in front of the very places he had been earlier in the day.

There were bullet holes everywhere he had run. Spanish Fly was literally watching his life play out on the T.V. and to him it looked like an old black and white World War II movie. The bedroom door opened.

"Y'all only can stay for a while," Sweety said agreeing to give them temporary room and board. Spanish Fly reached in his pocket and pulled out a stack of hundred-dollar bills and sat it on the table as a gesture of thank you. Then he removed himself from the kitchen and laid out on Sweety's couch without another word.

CHAPTER 11

The lawless, hard hearted, unorthodox criminals were housed on the compound separated from the general population of the prison. Every cell on the cell block that was occupied had an animated character behind its steel door.

Disposed to a small concrete and steel prison cell with the number sixty painted on the door. He laid down on the cold floor and elevated his feet onto the steel bunk frame. Inmate R000815 spent countless of vindictive nights virtually staring up at the ceiling. Tattoos inked all over his face and body told the unique story of his life. He pushed his body up by his arms off the floor. "One," he counted and then let himself back down to the ground slowly. "Two-Three-Four." Every day at the same exact time, he performed the same routine to sculpture his body like a Greek statue.

His muscle structure was flawless. Being a prisoner and incarcerated for so long the state noise outside his door was normal to him. He could hear the gifted stud a few cell doors down from him named Ceno Bandz banging on the door trying to get everyone else to stop talking so he could have the floor. Once he gathered everybody's undivided attention, it was silent just like he needed it to be, all ears on deck was at the mercy of his will. The small mistral began to orchestrate his contained talent by spitting metaphors, rhymes, like he was performing on stage at the Grammy Awards.

They just wanna see me fold but I can't let these niggas.
Police workin' for control I'm like "Fuck" these bitches.
R.I.P. my homies gone but I know they with me.
My mama trippin' on the phone but I know she miss me.
I'm just reminiscing "Yeah" this get so stressful.
They just wanna see me fold but I can't let these niggas.
Police workin' for control, I'm like "Fuck" these bitches.
R.I.P. my homies gone but I know they with me.
My mama trippin' on the phone but I know she miss me.
I'm just reminiscing "Yeah" this get so stressful.
They really wanna see me down, I gotta hold my head up.
Judge steady freeing all these clowns, I know I can do better.
I know I'm something better, this .40 apple pressure.

Whenever the little stud was released, he was surely to make some noise on the music scene. The concert was closed when the main entrance door to the cell block flew open.

It became quiet on the deck. All the convicted felons except one came to the windows of their cells to see what was going on.

"On the New!" one inmate yelled and now it was on. They all were looking outside their cell doors at the two correctional officers bring in the shackled new arrival with pure malice in their eyes. A few habitual criminals felt the need to flash gang signals up in the small window of their cell doors. Twisting and curling their fingers, signifying their allegiance to their affiliations, and also letting the new arrival know exactly where they stood. The other guys in their cells were kicking and pounding on the steel doors making the place rumble. They all were yelling out profanities, taunting the correctional officers of the law. The police moved in a timely fashion to place the new resident in his living quarters so they could quickly gallop out of there. They closed the main entrance door behind them and it was business as usual on the block.

"Aye! Aye! Who dat in cell 59?" one of the prisoners yelled

out. Even for a new arrival, the atmosphere was old. This wasn't the new residents first time down. He went to the window of his cell door and looked out.

"Yo who dat? It's Wiggles." Like a true convict, he yelled back through the door and waited for a response.

"Awe! My boi, what's up? It's yo' boi Ceno Bandz. Damn, what tha fuck happened?"

The new inmate Wiggles shook his head and then dropped it in the window.

"Fuck!!" he yelled out through the door across the deck in frustration. Then he lifted his head. "I couldn't wiggle my way out of a jam, I had to pop ah mothafucka to get outta there and the police caught me running down the street with the gun my boi," he explained the short version of the story to the cell block on how he ended up living with them.

"Awe! That's fucked up mane!" Ceno Bandz yelled to him and then he continued with his dialogue, "Aye! Aye! Wiggles you hear me. Aye! What's been goin' on out there on the streets?" Ceno Bandz and everybody else on the cell block was quiet and listening closely, greatly anticipating what was about to be said next. They all wanted to know since they hadn't been with the shits in years.

"What! Y'all ain't heard my dude? Aye, you hear me my dude. You know that lil' mothafucka Small-Time out there. The lil' mothafucka making all the money in the projects on Fate Street." Then he paused to see if Ceno Bandz knew who he was talking about.

"Aye! Wiggles. Yeah, I heard about him. You hear me! But I don't know him!" Ceno Bandz yelled back from the other end of the cell block.

"Yeah well anyway him and his guys just bodied some old mothafucka last night. My man's told me this morning about this on the phone before they moved me over here. You hear me! Aye! And the lil' nigga Small-Time had it recording on his phone, while he was going live on the book. That mothafucka got over ah million views already and still racking up numbers. Aye! My dude check this shit out. He ain't even going to jail because the police said he didn't have nothing to do with the murder because the shit just so happened when he was putting the nigga on blast for snitchin'." Right when he got to that part, the main entrance door opened again, and Wiggles took the phone off the hook. The whole cell block became silent.

All three of them walked through the door. Like before every prisoner in their cell came to the small window of the steel door. Once again, they watched the correctional officers covering his nose with the white handkerchief from the foul offensive smell. He gasped and tried his best to keep from gagging, but his attempt failed.

"Hulp, ugh, old lord it smells horrible," the priest spoke in disgust. Even though this was part of his job, the ordained priest really disliked the condemned wing of the juvenile department of corrections. The energy level seemed evil, and it felt like he was walking through a septic tank. He did not know how any human being could endure the overwhelming stench. Some of what he saw there was unimaginable he thought. As they walked, the C.O.'s did cell checks also. They were making sure the inmates still were alive. One of the correctional officers saw something that caught his eye so he stopped and started pounding on the cell door. He called himself trying to intervene on a good time in cell marked number sixty-seven. The C.O. saw a lonely inmate having an intimate moment with himself. The inmate rapidly pulled and yanked on his swollen genitalia with no regard for the law, trying to discover some form of pleasure from within himself. Like the priest trying not to gag, the C.O. attempt to break up a happy home had failed. The inmate acted like the correctional officer wasn't even there and like a handyman continued with his handiwork. The C.O. walked away disgusted and a failure.

"Nasty son-of-a-bitch. Oh, sorry father for my language," the C.O. said forgetting he was with a priest.

The reason there was no taunting or kicking on the doors this time was because they saw the priest and that meant one of their family members was deceased. They were just watching and waiting to see which door he was going to stop at.

Being so wrapped up in his exercise ritual he never paid attention to what was going on outside his cell door.

"Twenty-one. Twenty-two. Twenty-three," he counted out loud to himself. The priest and the two correctional officers stopped in front of his home, and the C.O. banged on his cell door with a wooden night stick.

"Hey! In there, Inmate R-000815 get up and come to the door." The Police gave him a direct command. He stopped the exercise and stood up with sweat running down his face and bulky chest. When he saw the priest with the police, he became suspicious in nature because they had no reason for standing in front of his cell door. The C.O. moved, and the priest stood in front of his window.

"Come to the door son. Are you inmate #R-000815?" the priest asked him through the window. No words spoken, Inmate #R-000815 just shook his head yes.

"I'm sorry to inform you, son, but your father was murdered in the Noware Housing Projects on Fate Street last night. Did he go by the street name Bamboo? Because if so, it's him, son. Would you like for me to pray with you right now?" he asked.

"E-E-E-E-E-E!!!" he yelled through the cell block. Ceno Bandz like the rest of the prisoners, heard every word the priest spoke to inmate #R-000815.

"Small-Time and nem killed dude's pops! That's fucked up!" Immediately afterwards, the new arrival Wiggles got on his door and proclaimed loudly. At that point, the whole cell block started kicking and banging on the doors, cursing, and going wild. It became a mad house. The priest stood there watching through the window at the kid. Inmate #R-000815 stared back giving the priest a cold disdain look. He could hear Ceno Bandz still on the door yelling.

"E-E-E-E-E-E!" was all the kid managed to mouthed.

CHAPTER 12

Rain or shine as long as the earth spins and paper spend, there's always a way to make a dime. All it takes is for a person to use their mind and use their muscle for the grind. One thing known for sure, time was precious, and it wasn't into the bad habit of procrastinating. As the beef on the stove was simmering and the cleanest cars slid out the carwash off into the sunset, shimmering, all he wanted to know, was who was next. Being who he was, the man wasn't into slacking up or chilling. Tiger was out there seating hard washing cars to the shillings.

Macvicious put the tailored made alligator skin shoes on his feet on the concrete He stepped out the stylish imported Jaguar, real smooth, looking important. As he watched a different Tiger he used to know, putting a different type of work on the streets. "Yeah man, I see you. What's up with you Tiger? You ain't playin up here boi. You got these cars looking good. I see you looking good too, I guess you ain't fuckin' around with that bottle no more, I see," Macvicious told him, making an accurate observation.

Tiger stopped wiping on the car and wiped the beads of sweat off his brow, then he looked at Macvicious with a serious facial expression. "Hey mane, I can't be no pretender. I know what hinders my growth. I had to let the bottle go if I wanted to grow.

You know?" Tiger said, admitting to what had been holding him down so long in life.

Macvicious was about to make another statement, but his phone began to ring.

"Aye, Tiger let me see who this is real quick," he said and then answered his cell phone.

"Let's talk about it. Hello. Oh, oh, oh, yeah, yeah. I know," Macvicious replied back to whoever he was talking to, walking back to his car for some privacy. That when the owner of vessel, Tiger was currently cleaning came with a satisfactory look on his face.

"A'ight, A'ight, you did that. You got me clean Tiger," the owner said, handing him the currency for the cleaning service, he'd performed.

"Aye Tiger what up with you and this washing cars shit? What happened to the pen and paper shits you was on?" the owner asked. Tiger put the money he had handed him in his pocket and finished wiping a shine on the man's vessel. Tiger took into account what the man said and then spoke the truth.

"Dig, that was a different time, ah different place, mane. I ain't picked up a pen since the Penn," he told him.

Then he wiped on the car once more and with professionalism opened the man's car door to let him in his ride. The owner accepted the small gesture and hopped in the car. He gave Tiger a fist bump, closed the door, adjusted his seat, and drove off clean as a recovering addict. Tiger hadn't noticed but Macvicious had been standing behind him. For how long? He wasn't certain.

"Tiger, who was playboy?" Macvicious asked him.

"When he was locked up everybody called him Philly. I think he's from the East Coast or something. Real smooth dude though, real smooth dude," Tiger let him know about Philly's character.

"Real smooth dude huh? Yeah, okay if that's what you say it is, then that's what it is. So, I'm net on the wash? The sun is about to go down and I gotta get ready to make my rounds," he asked, letting him know that he was pressed for time.

"Yeah, I got you. Tell yo' girl to pull up over here," Tiger said, getting the water in the five-gallon bucket, ready for the next wash.

"My employee," Macvicious said correcting Tiger about the relationship between him and the Russian girl driving his car.

"Yeah, well tell yo employee to pull that mothafuckin' car over here mane, would ya?" Tiger said, and they broke out in laughter.

"Boi, you funny as fuck. Yeah, I'ma tell her to pull over here playboy," Macvicious said with a smile.

It's said that sleep was the cousin of death and he'd been laid up with death's cousin all day long. His resting period was over for the rest of the evening. He would've been looking for Popcorn to stop his breathing. Spanish Fly couldn't keep letting the man blow him down everywhere he went. Spanish Fly was tired of the bullets flying in his direction. If Popcorn kept on carrying on the way he was, it wouldn't be long before he didn't miss what he was shooting at, which was him. To conquer his nightmares and the street at the same time, Spanish Fly was going to have to kill two birds with one stone.

The A-A 12-gauge shotgun with the thirty-round drum was going to get the job done. It was time to drop Popcorn on the floor, it was an all-out war, so that meant operation perception and deception was in full affect. He sat in his means of transportation and looked at his watch.

"The carwash may still be open. It's 5:47, I still can get washed real quick," he said as he turned the corner heading it in the direction to get his ride purified.

He wanted to be clean when he did his dirt. Those carwashes Tiger handed out was addictive and Spanish Fly like everyone else had an addiction to glitter and gleam, even if death was around the corner. He still was going to get it cleaned.

"Hey, once again, good lookin', my boi. Here's a tip," Macvicious said handing Tiger a crisp fifty-dollar bill, pleased with the job Tiger did on his car, then he walked away and got in the back seat of his ride.

Tiger saw the Russian girls getting on their function as Macvicious sat down and closed the car door.

"So that's how that goes mmm. Some can and some can't," he said to himself watching his finished product merge into traffic.

Tiger was about to close shop when somebody pulled up wanting a wash. He was tired and his body ached, but he couldn't afford to pass up on the cash. He remembered how he used to be in the projects up all night trying to get it right. Dodging the police, trying to get it right. The truth was the game wasn't for him, so no matter what, he was never going to get it right and for him that was his truth.

"Whoa, Whoa, pull up right here," Tiger said guiding the vehicle where he needed it to be, so he could handle his business.

"Who is this," Tiger said once again to himself because the ride wasn't familiar to him and the dark tent on the windows prevented him from seeing who was driving.

The vehicle stopped where he pointed, and the driver side window slowly dropped. Tiger waited to see who was going to appear and wasn't surprised at all to see who it was.

"Awe mane, this ain't you. This don't fit you at all. This ain't yo style mane," Tiger boast, but from what he surveyed, he knew the score and buddy was trying to even up the score with this move.

"Awe, Tiger it ain't nothin'. Just something to move around in. Ya know, get me from here to there. What's up? I need you to get me clean though. You know how you do boi," Spanish Fly told him and handing out the blood money with a smirk. Tiger raised one eyebrow. Then he looked at the vehicle, then his eyes wandered over Spanish Fly's to see the other occupant of the vehicle sitting there with the intent to kill. Then Tiger looked back at Spanish Fly and took the money.

"From here to there huh?" Tiger repeated. Spanish Fly squinted his eyes at Tiger.

"Yeah, I hear Mercedes Benz ain't what's in this time of year no way," Tiger said sarcastically, then he felt the need to wrap the conversation up.

"Yeah, say, aye mane. Roll ya window up, my nig. This won't take long at all," he guaranteed Spanish Fly.

The tinted window slowly rolled up and Tiger took the water hose and began to spray down the vehicle with water. Being in the streets, he knew and seen how this was going to end up. Tiger finished spraying the vehicle and dipped the sponge in the bucket of soapy water and started with the cleaning process, making sure not to leave one fingerprint behind, for a crime scene investigator to be implicating him in any wrongdoing. As Tiger was doing his job, he seen the flame from a lighter inside the ride behind the dark tent. That only meant one thing, Spanish Fly was getting his mind right for the night.

Even though the windows and doors was closed, he still could smell the loud aroma of the drug Spanish Fly was inhaling as he was getting his lungs dirty with the best smoke known to mankind. Tiger could hear him coughing repeatedly trying to hold the smoke and his composure. That's when Tiger saw what Spanish Fly saw and in the nick of time too. He hurried up and jumped away from the vehicle as it bolted into traffic, halfway washed with soapy water flying everywhere and tires screeching out of the parking lot.

"Awe shit. Let me get this shit up and get the fuck outta here," Tiger said and that's when he heard four of five thunderous explosions off in the night. Even if you weren't from the streets, you knew what that was.

CHAPTER 13

"Mommy, Mommy, Daddy said he love you, Mommy," the three-year-old girl repeated what she heard from her loving father. Maybe too loving father who was in hot water with his wife.

"John, what am I supposed to say to my friend at work? What am I going to say to the people at our church, John? Huh? How am I going to explain to everybody we know that my husband, the father of my child's face is plastered on the local news and newspaper for being busted in a prostitution sting? Oh, and by the way nice mugshot John." The embarrassed thirty-eight-year-old middle-class white lady bickered in the gray Volvo station wagon, to her husband of twenty years.

"Mommy, Mommy, Daddy got bee sting, Mommy. Daddy got bee sting Mommy. Ouch bee sting hurt Daddy?" the little girl asked her father who was just bonded out of jail for solicitation.

"No darling, Daddy's perfectly alright honey. Okay let Mommy and Daddy talk. Look Mandy I'm sorry. I don't know how to explain this," he said with a deep sigh. From the looks of it, he'd looked like hell. His hair was scruffy, his business tie was unloosened around his collar, which had been stained with lip stick and he needed a shave. That's the time her emotions got the best of her, and Mandy broke out in tears.

"Oh, how could you do this to our family?" she said weeping

at the stop light.

"Daddy, Daddy, Mommy's sad, Mommy's crying," the little girl said from her car seat in the backseat.

"Mandy plea—" John was cut off by the loud music coming from the black Camaro pulling up to the red light on the left side of them in the turning lane.

"Oh, I hate when those hoodlums do this," John complained.

"John how could you do his to me? I love you and you go have sex with prostitutes and then come home and kiss our daughter with those lips you've been kissing on those nasty, filthy unholy women. John, oh, how could you?" Mandy continued to throw stones at him. The deep bass coming from the Camaro with the fancy wheels made their car vibrate. That's when John observed a white Chrysler Town & Country Touring Van parked at the lights in the right lane on the other side of them. John noticed something odd about the white van and thought he would bring a little humor in the car with what he saw.

"Wow honey, they must have really been in a rush. The car is halfway washed Hun. Wait, why are they opening the door? Ooohh! For Christ's sake get down honey!" John screamed as he watched the man with the shotgun exit the white van and run-in front of their car towards the black Camaro with the fancy shotgun.

Ba-Boom-Ba-Boom-Ba-Boom-Ba-Boom. Spanish Fly was working the AA twelve-gauge shotgun with the thirty-round drum like a pro. The black Camaro was being eaten alive by the gunshots. The back and side windows were blown out. The car doors were riddled with buck shots. He could see through the back window and Spanish Fly aimed at the back of the driver's seat Ba-Boom-Ba-Boom-Ba-Boom. The black Camaro began to slowly roll into the ongoing traffic where it was struck by a pickup truck and then spun around and collided into another moving vehicle before it stopped in the middle of the five-lane intersection.

All traffic came to a stop. People were exiting their cars with the shock value on their faces. Some heroic guys were running from their cars through the intersection on their way to try and save lives until they saw Spanish Fly running with the shotgun towards the demolished black Camaro. They quickly changed their minds and their direction. They couldn't do anything but stand at a safe distance and watch the horrific homicide take place.

Ba-Boom-Ba-Boom-Ba-Boom-Ba-Boom.Spanish Fly kept pumping and shooting at the crushed-up car. He was making sure this was it. The by standers watched in awe, the heroic guys just shook their heads in disbelief and hung up their capes. The person sitting in the black Camaro was beyond saving and whenever the emergency responders arrive, the person was going to be beyond recognition if the man continued to shoot him like that.

"God sakes, that's enough!" an angry bystander protested hoping Spanish Fly would cease fire.

Ba-Boom! He didn't care about the people's cry for mercy, but what he did care about was the police sirens approaching. He snapped out of his zone and entered back into reality. He backed up from Popcorn's car and looked around to see all the damage he had caused. He shot the gun in the air Ba-Boom! That was just in case someone had the bright idea of making a citizen's arrest. As he was running back to the van, Spanish Fly could see a man leaning over the steering wheel of his pickup truck bleeding and hurt pretty bad. Then he seen a lady bleeding in the other car that struck Popcorn's car before it stopped. He was now back at the white van, and he looked in the gray Volvo.

"Aye, I know you. I saw you on the news this morning in that prostitution sting my boi," he said laughing and then closed the door.

Spanish Fly placed the other vehicle occupant, with the killer intent back on the passenger's side and sped off through the intersection and disappeared like a magic trick. The people still there rushed to the pickup truck and the other car with the injured lady and began to assist them the best way they could until the real help came. The other people that could stomach the sight, just stood around and the black Camaro crossing their chests and shaking their heads.

"Mandy are you okay?" John asked over their daughter's screaming and crying on the floor in the back. She looked at her husband in shock.

"Honey are you okay?" he asked his wife again. Her eyes were puffy from crying, but the tears had stopped flowing down her rosy cheeks.

"That man said he knew you John. From the news. From the prostitution bust. I want a divorce John. A divorce," Mandy told her husband with a calmness.

"Wait Mandy you don't really mean that honey—" she cut him off.

"A divorce, John!" Mandy yelled as she pounded her fist on the steering wheel of the gray Volvo.

***

When Popcorn had finally awakened from what seemed like from the dead, the first thing he did was light up a cigarette.

"Ooh, what is this, damn this is nice." He picked up the Mac II with the silencer to keep everything low key. He held it up in the light of the television so he could do a thorough inspection of the machine gun.

"Awe yeah this what the fuck I'm talking about," he said, realizing the weapon was perfect for him. He dumped the ashes from the cigarette into the glass ashtray and saw a note laying on the table. He set the gun back down on the table and picked up the note and read it aloud to himself as he continued to sit on the couch and smoke the cigarette.

I didn't want to wake you up, but I bought you a present, so you can collect on your debt. And by the way give the big gun a lil more rest nephew. Popcorn sat the note in the ash tray and set it on fire. He picked up the machine gun again with a smile.

"Yeah, yeah Unc, going out for a pack of smokes got you smoked. They say bad habits is the cause of most deaths. Maybe that's why you felt the way you did about Spanish Fly. you always did say to always trust your instincts before you be extinct. I should have listened," Popcorn spoke aloud as if he was speaking to Seville.

CHAPTER 14

The *stray kat* found a safe place with her tail up, purring in the back of the store, while the imaginary archaeologist was taking pleasure in his search. She was letting him have his way and wanted him to know it.

"Unh-unh-yeah-babe-find it," she whined., while the old Jewish man wearing a fedora and no clothes on, stood behind her digging deep in his exploration. She laid face down with her breast smashed as she straight bent over the cold cast iron safe that was opened. The safe was a gold mine. It had contained all sorts of jewels which was worked and undisclosed amount of money.

"Oooh-Unh-yeah-Unh-find-your-treasure-Unh,"she moaned loud. He held her waist tight and kept on digging from behind penetrating with his shovel in hopes to find what he'd been looking for.

"Unh-unh-Unh-dig-in-there babe-ooh-keep-digging," she encouraged him to continue with his search, while her sticky paws continued to go through the open cast iron safe in search of everything she could find.

"Yesss-Yesss-ohhh-dig-babe-did-unh." Her body bounced off of him every time he plowed in, making a clapping sound. The old Jewish jeweler was playing out of his fantasy of a true-blue treasure hunter.

Her long straight hair was not turning curly from sweat. Her ass cheeks were becoming pink from the pounding and her paws were pinching out the safe. She was allowing the old man to dig through her tunnels as she funneled through his wealth. This was her talent; this was her gift. She knew how to lift a heavy load without using a forklift.

"Keep-digging-ohhh-keep-digging-I-want-you-to-find-it." She kept moaning with her sexy voice, looking back at him. She teased him with her tongue, licking her lips, provoking him.

"Unh, unh, yeah," she cried as she watched him spit in the hole he was digging in, loosening the area. The old Jewish jeweler continued with his behind closed doors recreational activities of digging him her retail committing sodomy and rebelling against the shall nots of his religion. He put two of his fingers in her mouth to play with her tongue and muffle her moans.

"Mmm-mmm-umm-umm." She wiggled her tongue around his fingers, and she could feel him behind her shivering with chills of sensation. Everything was hid from her heist and she knew with a few more plunges he was going to lose control of his shovel. So, she arched her back and helped him find what he was looking for because she was done with getting what she was looking for.

"Oooh-oooh-babe-you-find-it-ugh-ooh-yeah babe you found it." She moved her ass on him making the old man's body jerk with a discharge of his youth. She let him remove his shovel from her tunnel as she removed one more item from the safe. She smiled at him because she came out on top in this give and take situation.

"Babe come with me to the restroom, so I can wash you up before I go. You're all dirty from digging in the dirt." She grabbed him by his shovel and led him to the restroom so she could rinse off the soil.

CHAPTER 15

Twenty stories high in the sky a beautiful angle carefully watched over the dark land waiting on her man to arrive alive. This was her final call. Luv-Luv listened to the phone ring again with no contact

"Ugh, this is going, de mal en pis," she spoke with frustration in both languages, English, and French, hanging up the phone for the sixth time. Luv-Luv's green eyes gazed out of the window down into the bloody streets, where there was a war going on. Her body temperature was cold as ice, but her palms were sweaty. Her heart was pounding like it could explode at any minute. Luv-Luv's nerves had her wanting to jump off the edge. It had been hours since her other half had split. Something was wrong, Spanish Fly had been gone too long without them communicating over the phone. Luv-Luv stood there staring out of the window, now believing he was dead and gone.

Everything was all fucked up now. Life was supposed to be better for them without him, but Spanish Fly's friend refused to lay down in the ground. It was totally the opposite. Everywhere they went, he was popping up and they were having to lay down on the ground. Before they had to lay under the ground. Nothing had gone the way they planned, and now she was standing there staring out the window. Hoping she wasn't going to have to plan Spanish Fly's funeral for him. She was praying the other way around and Spanish Fly was still alive. She was hoping he had burned Popcorn to a crisp before the funeral arrangements were hers.

"Girl still no word from Spanish?" Sweety asked, like a true friend standing by her side no matter what. Sweety's words of concern went unheard. Luv-Luv's mind was on the track because the thoughts were racing. All she could do was wonder if these few precious minutes would add up to her last and final hours.

Sweety touched her on the shoulder and Luv-Luv almost jumped out of her beautiful skin startled.

"Ahh! Where you come from Sweety?" she said breathing deeply. Sweety looked into her eyes and embraced Luv-Luv with a hug.

"Girl everything's going to be okay. He's going to come back soon, alright. C'mon and let's have a seat over here," she told Luv-Luv walking over to the sectional furniture to sit down, and they both stopped in their tracks when they heard a key unlocking the door.

"That's him now," she said trying to put Luv-Luv's worries to rest. Spanish Fly flew through the door with speed, shutting it behind him as quick as it came open. Sweety and Luv-Luv screamed in fear that something terrible had happened to him.

"Spanish! What happened? Babe are you okay, babe are you hurt, did you get shot, what's wrong?" Luv-Luv said frantically rushing to his aid, patting him up and down his body looking for any evidence of an injury. He was trying to hug her, and she was checking for blood stains.

"Nah, I'm cool, I'm cool, but I got 'em," he told her and she froze up with a chill running through her soul. "You hear what I just said? I said, I got 'em," he repeated himself expecting a different reaction this time when he told her. But nothing changed. Her response to the supposedly best news of their life was the same. "Aye we gonna have to stay low for a while until the shit cool down. I got some money to pick up tomorrow and we outta here for a minute. So, I want you to get ready to move when I'm ready to move and right now I don't have time for questions. Just be ready to move when I move," he told her, walking to the sectional furniture, and flopping down so he could soak everything in that just happened.

Popcorn was no longer with them and now the streets belonged to him. He now wore the crown; he now was going to handle business his way without the whispers in the shadows about Popcorn. Sweety and Luv-Luv stood there in shock, it was total silence in the place. They still couldn't believe Popcorn had been erased and it showed on their face. Neither of them knew what to do from that point on. Sweety walked to her room and shut the door. Like a beautiful angel, she went back to the window and looked down on the dark streets and became overwhelmed with a sense of inner peace.

"A bientot, Popcorn." Luv-Luv grinned speaking softly at the window as the queen angel.

"Aye turn the T.V. on," Spanish Fly said breaking her peaceful moment. "I need to know what they talkin about." She walked and grabbed the remote control from the kitchen and came back to the couch and snuggled up next to her king. Luv-Luv pressed the power button and the room lit up from the television screen. "See if the new is on yet," he ordered and she began to channel surf until the channel he requested was located.

***

Peeking out of the black mini blinds there still was no sign of his uncle Seville. Popcorn walked back to the couch and had a seat. He leaned over and reached in the ashtray to retrieve a cigarette that had been put out halfway. He put the half of a cancer stick between his lips and sparked a flame with the black cigarette lighter laying on the table next to the Mac II. He slept the day away having dreams about sending bullets through Spanish Fly's thinking cap and leaving Luv-Luv's pretty little face blemished with the multiple gunshot wounds. He sat there trying to figure out what was really going on. Since everything happened, Popcorn never took the time to analyze the situation. He couldn't see Spanish Fly on his own, setting him up like that. Then he started thinking if Spanish Fly did come up with the brilliant plan of laying him down in front of an audience at church, how long had his so-called friend been wanting to do him in. Popcorn smirked at the thought and once again he stood up.

Popcorn was still smoking the cigarette as he began to walk back to the window for a quick peek out of the mini blinds again. On the inside he was feeling strange, Seville wasn't the type of man who played games. Popcorn hit the cigarette walking back to the couch. He sat down and put the cigarette butt out in the glass ashtray. Then looking at the Mac II Popcorn remembered something his uncle wrote to him when he was young and dumb. He sat back and let the memory play through his mind.

The fourteen-year-old Popcorn stood in the parking lot of the Noware Housing Projects on Fate Street. The teenager used two parked cars as cover while he stood between them trying to generate him some revenue.

"C'mon man hurry up. Either you want it or move around. The police been rollin' through this mothafucka all day," Popcorn said with urgency, looking around his surroundings making sure that he didn't see any unmarked detective cars circling the area. There had just been a police sweep and the projects was hot.

"Un-uh, Popcorn. I don't know if I wanna spend my money on this lil' shit. These is too small," the shady customer was telling him to finesse Popcorn out his goods.

"Man, you know what? Fuck this shit, I'm gone," Popcorn said, ready to unsuccessfully close on the deal.

"Wait, wait, now hold on one minute. Ain't no need for all of that Popcorn, my main man. I'ma spend witcha, but next time do me right, alright. We cool?" the shady customer said trying to convince Popcorn to make the deal.

The shady customers dirt bag antennas begin to rise as his yellow shifty eyes scanned all escape routes, and one had been selected. The old school shady customer had made his mind up to bust a move on the young whipper snapper in the battlefield.

"Yeah, mmm-hmm my man Popcorn always look out for a real player you did," he said bobbing his head and flashing the three only yellow teeth left in his mouth while handing Popcorn the counterfeit money in hopes to pull one over on the young man. Interrupting what was going on someone yelled out his name from behind him.

"Uh-oh! Popcorn what's up?" Popcorn turned his head at the same time the business transaction was transpiring. Popcorn looked surprised. "Spanish?" he said recognizing the boy's face he saved on the bridge a few days ago. The shady customer squinted his yellow eyes. He could see this was the moment he'd been waiting for. He found his opportunity to make a run for it and he was about to take off. His smiling face broke down to a frown, it was about to go down. "Awe, hell nah, mothefuc—" Popcorn knew by the feel of the money dude was on some slick shit and he'd been tricked.

When Popcorn spun back around, he was a day late and a dollar short. He seen the mean mug on the customer's face. All he could do was brace himself. The shady customer hauled off and kicked Popcorn in the testicles, testing out the old wore out construction boot. Then he made a run for it. Popcorn was not a victim of foul play. As he fell down to the ground in between the two cars, he still held on to the counterfeit money he received groping in serious pain.

"Uggh-umm." He had balled up on the ground with his stomach hurting. Popcorn coughed. He couldn't keep laying there. Popcorn had to get up and chase the money. "Aah, shit ooh mothafucka, Whoo mothafucka," he said pushing himself off the ground and putting the counterfeit money in his pocket. He knew it would come in handy somewhere down the line when it was his time to hand it off on someone.

"Hell, yeah get that punk mothafucka, Spanish!" Popcorn yelled with some excitement. When he saw Spanish Fly chasing the Shady customer through the brick apartment building and apprehending the man with the fisticuffs. Spanish Fly was letting his arms fly and landing punches accurately across the man's face. The shady customer was taking the solid blows like a champ and still being swift on his toes. That was until Popcorn caught up with them and got in on the action from kingdom come, Popcorn swung with his left catching the shady customer. Spanish Fly continued to let the punches fly all over the shady customer's face.

"Ooh-ooh-ahh-alright! Alright! Man stop!" the shady customer screamed, but it didn't seem to help at all. Popcorn and Spanish Fly couldn't hear his plea for mercy because they were too busy concentrating on the ass whooping, they were handing him.

"Aah-aah-c'mon-y'all-aah-shit!" His screams grew louder bringing forth a small crowd of people circling around them. Popcorn and Spanish Fly continued laying hands on the man in the worst way.

"Nigga-you-was-gonna-take-my-shit! Uh!" Popcorn interrogated him while still introducing him to his fist. Popcorn's anger had taken over him. He cocked back and punched the man so hard, that it broke the man's jawbone.

"Aahhh!" the shady customer yelled in pain while his mouth hung around freely. Just like seeing the light from every punch he was receiving, a light bulb lit up over the man's knotted head. In the middle of his ass whooping, the shady customer came up with the bright idea he saw from a dog. The man totally stopped screaming and moving. But that didn't deter them at all. Popcorn and Spanish Fly kept punching the shady customer with all the strength they could muster up, but he refused to move. Every time he got struck by a blow his body just flopped around. Spanish

Fly noticed he wasn't responding to his punches anymore, so he eased up. He stood there exhausted, watching Popcorn continue to handle his business all by his lonesome. Popcorn changed the interrogation into informing the shady customer about his store policy.

"Mothafucka! You ain't dead. Bitch! You hear me bitch? You hear me bitch? You better not ever try and take shit from me again!" Popcorn told him while the man was still absorbing every last one of the hard blows Popcorn was throwing upside his head making sure the information was sinking through. The shady customer could have won an academy award for best actor for playing the role. He laid stretched out with his arms and legs out in a puddle of blood without any sign of life.

"Mothafucka, unh," Popcorn grunted with his final punch of information. That's when a lady in the crowd gave the bloody motionless man her honest to God opinion from her standpoint.

"I betcha you ain't gonna do whatever you did no more. I betcha," she said with her little arms crossed.

The show was over, everybody dispersed and went back to minding their own business. As Popcorn wrapped up his business affairs, he began rummaging in the man's pockets to locate his merchandise and on his search, Popcorn found what he was looking for and more. It just so happened the man had real authentic money on him that he was trying to save.

"Awe! Bitch you got money?" Popcorn said in amusement. He looked around and picked up an empty beer bottle and struck the man with it, shattering the glass all over the man's head. That made the shady customer stop playing dead. When the bottle busted over his cranium, cracking his head open like an egg, he absolutely couldn't afford to keep taking that kind of abuse with a burst of energy he leapt to his feet and cut loose. The shady customer took off running dead into ongoing traffic. Almost getting himself struck by moving vehicles. They were honking their horns and swerving in the street to keep from hitting him.

"I knew that nigga wasn't dead. I could still see his ass breathing," Popcorn said laughing.

Spanish Fly on the other hand stood there still watching the injured individual who they'd severely beaten disappear without his boots across the street as he ran behind some vacant buildings. Then he turned and looked at Popcorn who continued to laugh while counting his money, which made Spanish Fly laugh.

"Watcha doin' out here dude?" Popcorn said breaking the laughter on a serious note. Spanish Fly stopped with the laughter too and tensed up.

"This ain't gonna be like last time, so whatever you wanna do, we can do it," said Spanish Fly. He let Popcorn know. Popcorn turned his back on him, then Popcorn put the bloody money he took from the shady customer in a separate pocket from the counterfeit money and began to walk.

"Aye man where you going?" Spanish Fly asked, walking along side of him.

"Home, don't you see this blood on me? I gotta change clothes." Popcorn gave him an answer. "C'mon, I gotta go right over here," he told Spanish Fly. The walk was short. "Wait right here, I'm coming right back."

Spanish Fly stood in front of the building where Popcorn lived in the housing projects. Popcorn opened the screen door to his apartment and walked in.

Popcorn's Uncle Seville was standing in the kitchen smoking a cigarette, when he entered the apartment looking out the door. Popcorn walked up to him.

"Aye Seville watch my friend standing right here, until I change my clothes real quick," he said on his way to go to change but was stopped in mid stride when his uncle grabbed him by the shoulder, making him spin around.

"What, Seville?" he mumbled under his breath. Walking over to the table, Seville took out a sheet of paper and Popcorn reached for the ink pen on the kitchen counter next to the refrigerator and handed it over to Seville. Popcorn waited impatiently while his uncle put the writing utensil to serious use. He paced back and forth to the door, only to look out the screen window to see if Spanish Fly was still posted up where he left him. Spanish Fly hadn't moved a muscle, he still was on location waiting on him. Then Popcorn turned around to see if his uncle was done writing and he was. Seville had handed his nephew the paper and Popcorn quickly and quietly read it to himself.

"You ain't got no friends." Popcorn stopped reading and looked up at Seville. Seville took a puff off the cigarette and blew out the smoke. Popcorn went back to reading the note written on the paper.

A friend is only a person waiting to be ya enemy. They use that friend shit to get close enough to do you harm. Make sure you never forget that. You can do what you wanna do but he ain't ya friend. Keep that lil' mothafucka away from me. I don't want him nowhere around me and when you come back I wanna know where you find him at because wherever you found him you should have left him.

CHAPTER 16

Some say give with a frown, take with a smile. One of the most difficult things to experience in life is to lose someone you love and have to let them go. Some people go insane because of the heartache and pain. Most, wish things could go back to the way they were. Then there are those who chose to hurt others, so others can experience the hurt they feel. Either way, the wrath stood right outside Popcorn's door ready to assist him.

Popcorn had spent most of the evening, chilling on Seville's couch, smoking weed. He was blowing out thick smoke and coughing hard. Trying not to let his lungs collapse as he relaxed on the couch. Laid back with the Mac II in his lap. He sat in a cloud of heavy smoke, not having any restrictions on how high he'd get. His glossy red eyes locked in on the television. There in the air he made the decision to neglect the no-fly high zone, warning signs before he realized there hadn't been any sign of his uncle Seville.

It wasn't until he watched the horrific footage streaming across the TV screen showing the police standing around his shot up and mangled car folded into a light pole. The moving narcotic smoke paused for the cause. His time frame became warped. The clock began to tick slow, and the room seemed to warm up immensely. No love, no heart, the world became dark.

It was as if he had left this earth and suddenly dwelled in hell. The television audio started dragging along making the sexy lady's voice who was reporting the news, sound, slow, deep with bass, and demonized.

"In today's cover story, the F.B.I. reported that Rockford, Illinois is the number one most dangerous small city in the United States of America and that very well may be the case. Right now, the Rockford Police are on the location of an all too familiar scene. They are investigating a case where a car has been riddled with numerous bucks shot holes from a shotgun making it crash into ongoing traffic and ending up wrapped around a light pole at one of the busiest intersections in town, leaving two critically injured inside of their vehicles and a sixty-three-year-old elderly man dead at the scene, with the busy street overpopulated with empty .40 shell casings. There have been more than 157 people shot this year and the number of shootings is steady increasing with another fatal shooting today at the busy intersections of Karma and Fate Streets, making this Rockford's 158th shooting and the city's fiftieth homicide to date. The city's law enforcement agencies are scrambling to gather information in efforts to solve another one of its city's gruesome and relentless violent crimes. The statistics show very disturbing data on unsolved homicides in the city. The numbers show only nine murders out of forty-nine have been solved, prosecuted, and sentenced. Once again making its distraught residents rethinking about, is Rockford a safe place to raise their children or should they put the for-sale sign in the yard and pack their suitcases and leave for a better place.

"Ha-Ha, Hmm, Popcorn so what's it gonna be." He was under the illusion the television was speaking to him.

There was a knock at the door and Popcorn got up to open it. There was wrath ready to oblige him in any and every way possible. At first it was treason, but now all that changed. The reason behind his killing season was much, much, more personal.

Regret, hurt, but mostly anger and vengeance was all wrapped up in the single tear not wanting to leave his red dilated eyes. The what-is and the what-ifs weighed heavily on his mind. This was all his fault. He was responsible for what he'd seen on the TV screen. Yellow tape adorned his wrecked car with his uncle slumped over the steering wheel, under the bloody white sheet with his leg hanging out of the car door.

There was no need of waiting for Seville anymore, he was gone and that was that. There wasn't going to be any coming back. His Uncle Seville had been murdered. He was dead and that was going to be something Popcorn would think about every night in his jail cell before he closed his eyes and went to bed. At that moment Seville's written words replayed in his head, *You can do what you want, but he ain't ya friend. Keep that lil' mothafucka away from me. I don't want him nowhere around me.* Popcorn went to stand up but couldn't. This loss was the cost of the game. Everybody had to pay to play and Popcorn was standing at the cash register now having to charge the brutal murder of his uncle to the game.

Emotionally wounded and high spirits falling from grace had left her with a bitter taste. The snuggling up heart felt kissing on his neck had stopped due to the top story on the local news. Unfortunately, the short-lived celebration came to a disheartening end. Spanish Fly and Luv-Luv both seen what inevitably couldn't be the be the truth on TV. The news reporter had fully misinformed the public on what really went down. His face felt heavy, his mouth hung opened, hoping what he'd just heard, and saw wasn't real. "Uh-huh, no, no, no Spanish!" Luv-Luv stood to her feet and paused, so she could poise herself, giving him an evil stare down. There was no need for canceling their tempers. They both knew point blank there was no getting around it. What aired on the news had just sealed their fate. At that very moment Sweety's bedroom door swung open and she appeared looking nervous.

"Hmmm okay, so what is y'all finna do?" she asked them with a concern for human life.

She knew like everybody who watched the news, if that wasn't Popcorn under them bloody sheets in the wrecked and shot-up Camaro on TV, then there was about to be a lot of candlelight vigils, funeral processions stopping traffic and repasses at churches in the surrounding area for days to come.

"Huh, so what's up girl? What is y'all finna do because I'm finna go. I just called some of my family out of town. Oh lord! I gotta get outta here. I gotta get away from y'all." Sweety ran back in her room and slammed the bedroom door. That little hysterical moment Sweety was having didn't make their situation any better.

Spanish Fly let out a deep sigh and dropped his head in his hands.

"Damn I killed Seville," he said under his breath and let out another deep sigh. Luv-Luv wasn't so sentimental or empathetic about the mistaken identity homicide. She paced around the place.

"C'est la guerre!" she screamed in French. Spanish Fly raised up off the couch, trying his best not to slap her. He knew now wasn't the time for that. The facts were the same, Popcorn remained and there was no question he still had to deal with him.

"I'm only going to say this once, I think you better, yet I know, you need to have a seat," he told Luv-Luv with a calmness in his voice, but with a look that meant, she'd better sit down because it was in her better judgment or have the police, coroner, and news reporter at Sweety's crib standing over her trying to investigate what happened to the beautiful woman.

Luv-Luv seemed to understand exactly where he was coming from and quickly took a seat on the couch. Besides the sound of the television, there was a silence in the place but that wasn't the case in Sweety's room. They could hear her ransacking through her dresser drawers and ranting to god, while she was packing suitcases getting ready to disappear for about a year until all the smoke cleared, then Spanish Fly broke the silence.

"You know this shit is all fucked up! Police is gonna be on my ass and I know this nigga is about to get on some real dumb shit. Baby girl I need you with me, not against me. Ya feel me? Where I need you, you need to be and that's right by my side. I love you. Do you love me because I need to know?" he asked her. Luv-Luv's face unfrowned and she looked at Spanish Fly with her watery green eyes.

"Ca va sans dier," she told hm speaking in a foreign tongue and taking him by his hand so he could have a seat next to her on the couch. Spanish Fly sat next to Luv-Luv being bound by some sort of spell.

"Let me tell you something Spanish, I love you," she said, leaning in and placing her soft lips on to his. "Mmm, mmm, I love you, Spanish," Luv-Luv moaned seductively.

They kissed, remembering the personal passion belonging to them. Spanish Fly embraced her sweet warm soft luscious lips as though it would be his last time kissing her in his life. She put her little hands on his chest and gently eased him back. She saw his eyes still closed and he was wrapped in the moment. Right then Luv-Luv felt his love for her.

"Mmm, Spanish baby you don't gotta worry about me, I'm going to be right here by your side. Promise you I'm not gonna go anywhere. You hear me my love?" Luv-Luv spoke softly gazing in his eyes touching the man's soul. He sat there mesmerized listening to her soothing voice. He blinked and quickly stood up breaking out of the trance he was under.

"Uhm, yeah. Look I thought I'd be old when I gave this to you," he said, being rudely interrupted by the loud ring from his cell phone sitting on the arm of the couch. Luv-Luv went back in mode, her attitude reappeared, and her beautiful face frowned up with anger.

"Answer ya phone Spanish," she said in a sassy fashion. He

looked at her like she was crazy.

"Look girl I'm trying to tell you something right now and you sitting there talkin about the mothafuckin phone. I don't give a fuck about a phone! If that's so mothafuckin important to you then you gone and answer the mothafucka." Before he could finish giving Luv-Luv permission to answer his phone, she hurried and grabbed the phone.

"Hello," Luv-Luv said answering the phone trying to be nosey but was taken by surprise from what she was hearing on the other side. "Uh, hello, hello, who is this? Hello, can you hear me? What's wrong with you?" she said to the person on the other end of the phone. Now looking at Spanish Fly like he was crazy, his face began to frown up.

"What the fuck is you looking at me like that for? Who tha fuck is it?" he asked her becoming angry. Shrugging her shoulders, Luv-Luv looked puzzled handing over the cell phone to him.

"It sounds like somebody's crying or something. I don't know who this is," she told him with her eyebrows raised and still confused. Spanish Fly stood there staring at the phone in his hand and then glanced back at her. He turned his back on her and walked over to the window overlooking the small city of Rockford. He could see as he looked down on the streets. Red and blue lights on an ambulance truck moving quickly in the night, either going to help or coming from trying to get some real help at the hospital.

He put the phone to his ear, "Who the fuck is this playin on my phone?" Spanish Fly could hear someone sobbing on the phone. "Man, aye whoever tha fuck this is, quit playin on my mothafuckin' phone," he said hanging up the phone. Then he went back to having the serious conversation with his woman before he was interrupted by the prank call cutting him off.

Death on his brain, his location had changed. Alone he sat in the pitch dark at his home pitching a fit. The pain was draining his body. Memories flashed through his mind like a picture show with him never picturing it ending like this. In the darkness his heart pounded with hate. His emotion fluctuated from sadness to pure madness. The guilt and grief wouldn't give him any relief. His stomach hurt from his soul being empty. His muscles tensed from tension. He couldn't believe the tenacity of someone whose life he had saved, repaying him back like this with death. His chest felt heavy, and breathing was short and fast. Popcorn sat there and dialed Spanish Fly's number again. This time, this particular phone, there would be no room for possibilities. Spanish Fly was going to know exactly who it be, that couldn't help but to call him back. He sat listening to the phone ring until it went to voice mail. Popcorn didn't want to leave or hide behind a text message. Popcorn wanted Spanish Fly to hear the pain in his voice, he was responsible for. Popcorn pressed send on his phone again and listened to it ring in his ear until it went to voicemail.

"Hi, the subscriber you are calling can't except any voicemails at the moment please call back another time," he was told by the automated operator. Popcorn's blood was boiling. He couldn't wait to see Spanish Fly for the last time. Popcorn dialed Spanish Fly's number once more and this time he heard Spanish Fly answering again, acting like he didn't know who it was calling his private phone line.

"Bitch ass nigga. You know I ain't playin', you know exactly who tha fuck I am, and I know you hear me. I'm killing you wherever I see you!" Popcorn was satisfied and he ended the conversation on that note.

Chills ran through Luv-Luv's body as she sat on the couch trying not to panic. She watched Spanish Fly's color complexion while he was listening to the phone call. He paced around in circles, yelling into his phone.

"Hello! Hello!? Fuck you nigga! Hello!" yelled Spanish Fly into the phone.

Sweety burst out the bedroom with her two suitcases stuffed with stuff.

"Girl y'all can stay here if you wanna but I'm gone tonight. I'ma call you when I get to where I'm going. Girl you know I love y'all. Hmmm, hmmm, like I said I'ma call you okay? Please answer your phone," said Sweety as she swept by Luv-Luv with no hugs or nothing.

CHAPTER 17

The damage was done, and something had to be done. This wasn't the first time the Rockford Police Department's top priority involved two renowned high-profile suspects. The two mug shots of Popcorn and Spanish Fly plastered on the bulletin board had been responsible for leaving empty shell casings and bodies scattered around the city as evidence that their tight lipped, close knit criminal enterprise did exist. The stories they heard about Popcorn and Spanish Fly wasn't just being manufactured out of thin air. The whole investigating detective unit knew firsthand the danger in having past dealings with the two cutthroats.

The question was, how many confidential informants lost their lives trying to infiltrate the two, only to get close enough to get smoked, having their brains knocked outside of their heads and exposing the failed undercover police operations called "Go back and think that over." How many houses had they raided and busted people for manufacturing and delivering within a thousand feet of a school with absolutely no one willing to corroborate and roll over to deliver Popcorn and Spanish Fly to them. The criminals all stuck to the rule. They were willing to go to jail rather than tell or end up like the other deceased confidential informants. The police knew these new open cases was something totally different. The shootings and yesterday's murder might have been the big break they so desperately needed. Something definitely was going on and that something was going to work in favor of the law.

Out of respect for the law, there was a lot of *good morning greetings* in the conference room that really wasn't so. An empty box of donuts and an out of order sign taped on the coffee maker was a clear indication that the morning wasn't so good, and it would be a long stressful day for each and every last one of the officers bunched in the room, especially those who came to work with a hangover from last night's open bar activities. Hangover or not every cop sitting there had a *hard on* for the two. Most of the guys in the conference room had climbed up through the ranks making arrest in connection with Spanish Fly and Popcorn's criminal conduct one way or another over the violent years.

The violence had been the same violence known throughout the low-income communities for over a decade. The citizens and elected officials tolerated it while the police turned a blind eye on the matter. As long as crime stayed withing the gun lines, then everything was fine. That meant you had a free pass to rob, kill, steal, rape as long as it all stayed within the gun line. Yesterday's homicide happened on the wrong side of the bridge where the community leaders played outside with their grandkids. The violence had transgressed the gunline into the upscaled neighborhoods of the community. Where now violence was a problem, and something had to be done about it. In this meeting today the proper authorities all came together to undergo strategic ways into bringing down Spanish Fly and Popcorn.

"Alright! Alright! Can I have everyone's attention?" the gray haired, short, chubby police commissioner made the announcement to bring the small talk to an end.

The short, chubby white man stood at the podium in his crisp, starched, blue uniform with the left side of his chest decorated with medals of valor classifying his expertise in the field.

"First I would like to thank the mayor of this city and the few aldermen for making this meeting this morning on such short notice," said the Commissioner.

The mayor and the few aldermen could have thought of a better place to be than spend their morning being there. The truth was they had to save face. It was an election year, and a lot of elective's seats were up for reelection. There were a few ne candidates on the ballot and the old ones needed to restore their reputation with the public, so the votes would tally on their behalf. The game was cold but fair. Some chose the streets to eat, while others chose, the elective seat. The public outcry for peace on the streets wore heavy on the young mayor's brow. As he sat there with a headache, preparing himself to listen how the police department were going to solve this problem between Popcorn and Spanish Fly.

The homicide yesterday in the upscale community had the public in fear. His phone rang off the hook all night about what had transpired. If something wasn't done soon about the incident, then his votes and job would be greatly threatened.

"And I also would like to say marvelous job to the guys involved in setting up the prostitution sting two nights ago. You guys really made the department look good on the news, so once again, great job and keep up the good work," he praised the detectives for their accomplishment in nabbing ten women for prostitution and twenty men for solicitation.

"On the other hand, let's get down to the real reason we are all sitting here so early in the morning," he said and then turned around so he could point his stubby index finger at the bulletin board.

"We're going to bring these two sons-of-bitches down before the sun sets in the west." The police commissioner seemed to be stealing lines from an old western movie.

The detectives sat there listening to the commissioner rant and rave about the public and politics, trying to make himself look good for the mayor and company as their eyes analyze the square brackets connection other criminals in the streets to Popcorn and Spanish Fly. They were following the lines, making comparisons between crimes and photos trying to link everything together. Some of the criminals on the bulletin board had two photos of them taken, maybe because those criminals were just that bad or it just could have been a picture before when they were full of life, then a picture taken of them after life had left them and moved on to a better place for fucking around with Popcorn and Spanish Fly. Their eyes moved along other lines on the board putting together times and dates.

The commissioner was done with his opening speech and the debate was on. The detectives began arguing back and forth amongst each other trying to make logical sense of the details being presented before them and through all the commotion. There still was no witnesses or hard-core evidence placing a smoking gun in with of Popcorn or Spanish Fly's hand. The mayor listened with confusion written on his face. He couldn't believe the things he was hearing. He wanted to donate his two cents worth of opinion on the topic, but it was more of a question than an opinion. "Wait, wait a minute. You mean to tell me it's just these two guys who put a stronghold on the criminal world in my city? These guys are behind all the murders and drug activity and now they're feuding with each other?!I mean why now? Why would they feud with ea—"

The police commissioner cut the mayor's show short and took the floor giving him a disdainful look. Then he gave the mayor his honest opinion.

"Mayor, sir. I could give to shits why or have a clue to why these two sons-of-bitches are trying to kill each other. My job is to get them off the streets. Quite frankly you shouldn't be asking questions like that sir. All I'm concerned with right now is our chance to bring these two down," said the commissioner.

The room was quiet for a few seconds. Everyone was looking

around at each other waiting for the mayor to make a rebuttal, but the mayor was out of his league on this one, so he declined.

"Hmm, very well commissioner as you were," the mayor said and sat back and folded his arms across his chest and continued to listen.

The audience in the room bickered and argued in frustration on how to catch Popcorn and Spanish Fly. Emotions were flaring up and time was winding down. The central air blew crisp cold air through the ventilation system. Bringing temporal relief on the heated topic, on how to catch public enemy number one and two.

Not wanting to be there in the first place, the mayor's own frustrations started to set in. He exhaled deeply and looked at his watch on his wrist checking the time. This was only one of many meetings he had to attend today on his busy schedule. There were other important city matters, he had to deal with throughout the course of his day.

He had a nine o'clock meeting at his office with his administration about the county's deficit and then moving right along to ten. He had a groundbreaking ceremony to attend to attend for a new juvenile detention center being built in hopes of keeping the community safe. Then he looked over at the faces of the aldermen trying to hold down their early morning breakfast in their weak stomachs. They were only seconds away from vomiting on the class conference table after listening to horror stories over, and over about the violent crimes the tow criminals committed. Then having to sit there getting to see every detail being depicted in the gruesome crime scene photos of the blood aftermath Popcorn and Spanish Fly left behind. They too looked like they were ready to bring this meeting to an end and let the police do what the police was paid to do.

The mayor was about to politely excuse himself from the meeting when an elderly lady wearing her reading glasses at the tip of her nose, entered the conference room and tiptoed up to the police commissioner's. She handed him a piece of paper and whispered in his ear. Then she was back off to where she came from. The mayor took that to be the police commissioner's secretary. He smirked at the idea that she must have started working as a secretary for the police department when the commissioner was just a cadet in the police academy and over the years, they did more than just whisper and pass notes to each other.

"Son-of-a-bitch!" the police commissioner made an angry outburst.

After carefully reading whatever was wrote down on the small piece of paper handed to him by his secretary. The arguing and bickering detectives came to a pause. The aggravated mayor watched with cautious eyes as the police commissioner's temperature seemed to boil and his face became flushed.

"Uh, commissioner, what is it?" the mayor curiously asked.

The commissioner placed both hands on the podium to ease his stress, then he turned his head and looked directly at the mayor making sure he had the mayor's full attention. Before he became the barer of bad news, the commissioner let out a deep breath.

"Detective Whitaker," said the commissioner.

Everyone in the conference room turned and looked in his direction. The detective's heartbeat sped up; he could hear his co-workers whispering to each other. He could only imagine the things being said in the room on the low-key. Detective Whitaker wasn't a dirty cop but he also wasn't the cleanest. His eyes ran around the room trying to figure out which one of his co-workers had some dirty on him and had the audacity to rat him out. Whatever the commissioner was about to accuse him of. He was sitting there already thinking of the perfect alibi.

"Um yes sir," the detective replied with sweat pouring from underneath his baseball cap with the word "Police" on it. Then the commissioner proceeded to ask his question.

"Detective Whitaker, do you remember the name of lady you questioned at the beauty supply store about the shooting there?" the commissioner asked.

The detective became relaxed, and his anxiety left. When he come to learn, he wasn't the one under the microscope.

"Yes sir. Her name was um, wait one minute, let me get my note pad. Ah here it is, her name is Alecia Jenkins. Now that I remember, she was very nice and polite, but she kept her lips sealed. She wouldn't give any kinda information about the shooting the gunmen, I mean not a peep sir," he briefed the commissioner and looked over the faces in the room, then he began to speak again.

"Well, it seems, a newlywed couple, on their way to board a bus heading for Las Vegas, happened to find a young woman sitting in her vehicle deceased, so, they immediately called the police. The young woman has been unofficially identified as someone known as Sweety," the commissioner briefed everyone in the conference room. That caught everyone's attention.

"Un-fucking believable! She didn't deserve to be murdered! She wouldn't give me anything. She kept her fucking mouth closed. She didn't tell on anyone and now she's dead. Un-fucking believable!" Detective Whitaker yelled slamming his police logo baseball cap to the floor in disbelief.

"The responding officer said he walked up to the motor vehicle and investigated, the white Chrysler Town and Country Touring Van in the parking lot of a bus station, the African woman, sat slumped in the driver's seat unresponsive. He immediately recognized her and assessed the woman was deceased. He took the liberty to open the driver's door and identified her body covered in bloody money, in what later was determined to be in the amount of $3,000.00. He did a quick analysis and also discovered she bore a tattoo that read sweaty, uh I apologize, it read Sweety," the commissioner said as he continued to address the room.

"Those motherfuckers are animals. They didn't have to kill her!"

CHAPTER 18

It was Tiger's day off from the car wash, but he was still at work.

Clink—Clink---Clink---Clink. Sounded the metal against metal. Tiger lifted the steel weights, each time he pressed, making music as they sculpted his muscles into perfection. Tiger was giving it his best, trying to prevent his little ones from traveling down the rough road of crime and recidivism, like he did. How could he explain this mess? The only way he knew how to make sense of this world, could cause you to lose your sense and cents, figuratively speaking. He was exercising their little minds and their bodies at the same time as his sons watched him and listened to what he was saying.

Tiger thought he was giving it his all, although he knew his sons were going to see the wicked world for themselves, all he could do was make recommendations to keep them from being bagged up like a product. The way Tiger saw it, they could either be bagged by the police on the corner or bagged up off the ground by a coroner. Tiger didn't want his sons being the cornerstone of the new prisons and communities being built, so he was laying down a foundation by dropping the encyclopedia of the streets in their little ears. Tiger rapped with them about prison out dates and spoke about the memories. Tiger's purpose was to remove the hocus-pocus and get his sons to focus on the endangerment of a man with no education. As a father of many mistakes, Tiger was certified to provide the proper knowledge that would inspire a desire in them to go outside of the boundary lines that was set as an objective to keep them in the negative. Tiger put the 225 pounds of steel back on the rack and sat up on the old steel weight bench.

"Ahh, yeah, now where we at?" he asked.

Tiger new exactly where the conversation was, he just wanted to see if his little ones were paying attention and following along. All three of his sons resembled him physically but Tiger wanted their characteristics to resemble his current righteous mentality.

"It's fair to be square, they don't worry about the police and getting locked up because everything they do is legit," said one of Tiger's sons.

"Dad you said squares don't care when the police pull up on their bumper because they drive with license and insurance. Then you said a square can own any kind of gun they want because they never been arrested, because they was able to get a valid gun card," his son Kortae said.

Kortae, Tiger's oldest, stood six foot four inches and loved to show his awareness. Tiger nodded his head and was pleased with his son's accurate response. Tiger stood up and walked into his garage and came back out handing each one of his sons a set of dumbbells, he felt they could lift along with giving them the gift of game to make his boys three wise men.

"Okay well let me ask y'all this," Tiger said watching the veins bulge out of their little arms, while they were working out.

"Which would you rather do? Shoot dice made from toilet tissue in a jail cells for noodles or roll dice at a casino for money with a bad honey blowing on your dice for luck on your days off from work when you clean yourself up, looking good and feeling good, huh?" Tiger asked them, anticipating their response.

"The casino, Dad," they answered all at once.

They had finished doing their set of ten reps. Ambition

sometimes will make you want to take on a task you can't physically bare, even though you may think and feel like you can do it.

"Dad I'm tired of lifting these lil ol weights. I wanna lift that," his second son Lil' Tiger boldly said.

Standing at five feet six inches at the age of twelve, pointing to the 225 pounds sitting in the rack on the old weight bench. He was eagerly ready to put the laws of physics to the test.

"Lil' Tiger I hate to tell you when you can't do something, but son you can't lift that right now. That would be like putting the weight of the world on your shoulders. Son give yourself some time and trust me you will be able to handle that and the world. Just listen to what I tell you," Tiger said.

Just as he was about to collaborate with his youngest son Domonic, Tiger's parole officer pulled up in a white chevy Impala like he was warmly welcomed and parked in Tiger's driveway. Everybody had debts and Tiger was no different, he still had to pay his full debt off to society. Tiger's sons looked at him and then at his parole officer watching the man as he sat in the car making the proper adjustments to his bulletproof vest and service pistol before getting out of the vehicle to check Tiger's temperature.

"Aye, y'all go in the house and wash up. I'll be in there to check on y'all in a minute," Tiger said.

Tiger mentally noted he had been interrupted from teaching his children some ethical values, while he himself was *hanging on a chain* by due process of the law according to the State of Illinois, the parole officer was checking up on one of their best products.

CHAPTER 19

He rode in silence only listening to his thoughts. It was mandatory that he found Spanish Fly and lay him down today. Popcorn was being under the influence of death and was not yielding his actions on the mass destruction he was about to inflict. In the gray cloud of narcotic smoke, Popcorn was sick, and his blood shot eyes lacked mercy for the living. He was thirsty, but it wasn't from cotton mouth. Popcorn was riding around the streets in the all-black T-Top Chevy Camaro ready to initiate gunplay. The flycatcher sitting in his lap was guaranteed to leave his prey motionless on a stretcher. Behind the black tinted windows Popcorn never flinched or worried about getting pinched. He moved around corners stealthily, he had already passed several police cars in early morning traffic, he was itching to put Spanish Fly in a suit, make up and casket.

As Popcorn passed by the housing projects on Fate Street, he could see his new employee Small-Time and a few other businessmen, out there standing in the area where only days ago he had performed the appalling dental work on the convict. They were being careful networking and making physical efforts to get to the money, so they could boost their individual net worth. They were approaching cars driving through, supplying them with goods and getting them gone so the next customer could get taken care of with the good stuff.

Popcorn shifted gears in the black Camaro reminding himself not to forget to check on the little guy.

Popcorn inhaled more smoke, then he smashed on the gas and dashed down the street. The engine revved up sounding like an aircraft. Popcorn flew around the block and decided to take it upon himself to check on his work right now. He slowly turned into the projects on the street where Small-Time and the businessmen were posted up. He could see them trying to figure out who the hell it was. Popcorn continued to travel at a slow place with a smirk on his face. He knew they were out there talking about, should they shoot or run. The needed to make up their minds quick, but it was too late. Popcorn had stopped the car in front of them and let the passenger window roll down slightly. The smoke rushed out of the small crack in the window. Popcorn could hear their approval of the aroma exiting his vehicle.

"Yo, Small-Time! Let me holla at you real quick my boi," Popcorn called out to him from the car behind the thick smoke and dark tint.

Even though they didn't know who it was yet, everyone around Small-Time looked relieved that it was him and not them being summoned to the black Camaro. Small-Time recognized the voice but he wasn't quite sold on who or if it was the person he thought it was, so before he'd move one tennis shoe, Small-Time had to make sure.

"Yeah what's up? This me, is that you?" he responded.

Popcorn grinned nodding his head satisfied with the little kid and how he was conducting himself out there. Popcorn pressed the button to let the window come down completely. The smoke was leaving and the people standing around with Small-Time felt the need to do the same. They all knew Popcorn and everybody who knew what Popcorn, knew what he was on. They'd rather hear about the murders than to be there and see the murders in person. In their minds, this was the nigga, sitting in the black Camaro in front of them, that had the local news and social media going up in a frenzy. Small-Time wasn't like everyone else. Unfortunately, he was just a pawn in something much bigger than his four-foot ten-inch frame.

"Awe man, where you been? It's been so much money coming through here and I didn't know how to find you man," Small-Time said, walking up to the car.

Not even a split second before his little eyes, he became aware of the Mac II with the silencer sitting in Popcorn's lap.

Popcorn looked at him. "Is that right. You've been lookin' for me, huh?" he said.

Small-Time looked back over his shoulders real quick, he was trying to be slick, to see who out there had love for him and would stick around while their conversation was going on. But only to see, there wasn't a soul outside. Seems, they had remembered just like he did what happened the other day with the muscle-bound convict.

"Shit," he mumbled under his breath and then he looked aback at Popcorn.

"You still having problems with that nigga? Is he still talkin about his mama and where you can conduct ya business?" Popcorn asked Small-Time with genuine concern about his employee's work environment. Small-Time smiled at the question being asked because any person in their right or wrong mind wouldn't be saying nothing about where he could sell after what they saw.

"Uh, naw. I think he straight," Small-Time said.

Popcorn took a puff and held the smoke in his lungs as he continued to touch bases with Small-Time

"Yup, so you ain't see ya big homie Spanish Fly since the last time we talked, my boi?" Popcorn was talking to him still holding the smoke in his chest, then he exhaled.

"Huh? You ain't talked to him?" he continued to ask. Answering the wrong way, could mean closed curtains, show over.

"Small-Time," the little guy was saved by the supply and demand. It was a customer calling his name demanding to be supplied.

"Nope I ain't seen him. Look, I gotta go take care of this. Can you come back in an hour?" Small-Time said hoping this would get the conversation to end before he came to an untimely end.

"Yeah, no problem, I can do that sir. Aye, I'ma slide down on you later and we can hit a few blocks. You need to get out the projects sometime sir," Popcorn said.

Popcorn rolled up the black tinted window. The engine revved up and Small-Time watched the rear tires spin in place, then the car started to spin around in a full circle twice in the middle of the street. The only time the kid seen something like this was on tv. The whole street was becoming smoky, and Popcorn was in the car handling the wheel showing off his driving skills as his came out the spin. The car tire smoked and peeled all the way down the street and out the house projects. Popcorn left his signature in the street from the tire marks. Small-Time and the customer watched the stunt show until the black Camaro disappeared and then watched how everybody hat disappeared, reappear, asking all types of questions and acting like they were concerned for his well-being.

"Small-Time, what happened? You cool? What Popcorn say?" Small-Time served his customer and gave the customer a blessing because it was a blessing how he was right on time to get him out of that bind, then it was time to give a small press conference for all those who were asking questions with their scary asses.

"To answer y'all first question, naw, I ain't cool. Where y'all go? Then if you wanted to know what he said, y'all mothafuckin' asses shoulda stayed here and listened. And to answer the third question, ain't shit happened, but y'all scary mothafuckas leaving me!" Small -Time said, heated.

It was showtime. He pulled out his phone and went on social media live.

"What's up, what's up? I'ma tell you what ain't up. These scary mothafuckas right here," Small-Time said.

Small-Time took the camera off himself and put it on the people out there who left him, then he continued commenting and focusing the camera on the crowd, not begin discreet on who he was recording, but being very discreet about who left the tire marks in the street. When he pointed the camera in that direction.

"I ain't gonna say who just did this in the street, but what I'm gonna tell you is don't have none of these niggas around if somethin' goes down. Just like them tire marks in the street, that's how its gonna look when they tennis shoes start running down the street. Ha, ha, ha, ha. Awe man they took off on me," Small-Time said still giving the public facts on how everybody scattered out on him.

After the stunt show, Popcorn was back to looking for Spanish Fly, so he could get what little business he had with him over with.

CHAPTER 20

The weather didn't know whether to stay sunny or cloudy, but in the distance, it could be seen that more clouds were soon to make their arrival know and make the sun be gone. Spanish Fly was beginning to fully understand, the concept of what it cost to be the boss. He made move that seemed to be costing him everything. Last night the news broadcast and gossip on social media was going to have a lot of people gunning for him. Before they went on the run things needed to be done. He looked to his side on the ride and watched his beautiful goddess drive. Spanish Fly had Luv-Luv doing the job of escorting him around town to pick up funds on a money run. Through all of the choppy moments, at least he still had his love in his corner holding everything together. He was feeling down in the dumps. Being under the influence of a mistaken identity murder his natural character was deeply affected every time he put the $200.00 bottle of champagne up to his lips to take a sip trying to numb the pain.

"Ahh," was the sound he made from the satisfaction of drinking sparkling crushed grapes. Then he chased the sparkling grapes with the smooth and soothing taste of a $1000.00 bottle of aged cognac. The gun metal .357 snub nose with the wood grain handle was tucked in his waistline under his shirt, waiting for publicity. It wasn't alone either because the AA12 gauge laid next to Spanish Fly's leg in the passenger seat wanting another breath-taking appearance. Spanish Fly sipped more of the aged cognac from the glass bottle again. "Ahh." Then he pointed.

"Pull over, right over there." Spanish Fly gave the navigation for Luv-Luv to pull the vessel over.

They came to a stop and parked in front of a brick two story apartment building with a lot of suspicious activities going on. Automatically Luv-Luv became uneased.

"Spanish you finna be long?" she asked, as she continued to look out the window at potential trouble. He took another swig of cognac.

"Ugh, shit. Uh nope. Nope. In and out," he replied, wiping his mouth and opened the car door to get out still holding on to the champagne.

"Un-uh wait baby, let me hold that bottle for you until you get ba—" Luv-Luv's pleas were met with the door slamming in her face.

Spanish Fly was off balance as he walked crooked up to the red brick apartment building stumbling passed people and staggering through the open screen door.

"Vive le roi," she said in French shaking her head in disappointment.

To stay safe Luv-Luv pulled her pink .380 automatic pistol from her purse and sat it in her lap just in case she had to church somebody. To protect herself she had no problems catching a body. She wasn't about to be caught slipping while Spanish Fly was off his square sipping. To take her mind off the situation, Luv-Luv grabbed her cell phone and called her best friend Sweety. The cellphone was to her ear, but her green eyes were watching every single thing moving outside the car. The phone just rang and rang.

"C'mon, C'mon Sweety please answer the phone," she said in hopes her friend would pick up the phone and answer it.

Luv-Luv never got an answer, only the voice mail, so she called her friend again. Once again, she was getting the same result expecting something different.

"C'mon Sweety, I know you mad at me, but damn answer the phone, girl so I know you're alright," Luv-Luv was saying to herself, but still paying attention to the foot traffic, going in and out of the apartment building Spanish Fly entered.

The phone just rang and rang and rang. But was the same thing. She got Sweety's voicemail, so she hung up the phone and began to ponder on what was keeping Spanish Fly so long, then she decided to send a text message. Her French manicured fingers went to typing.

"Sweety please forgive me for everything, I didn't mean to pull you in so far in this mess. You're my best friend and I'm so sorry and last night well, I shoulda left with you. Spanish is— but anyway, have you left town yet? Are you on the bus? Please let me know something girl." Luv-Luv's fingers stopped typing, then she pressed send. Her anxiety level was at an all-time high and all she could do was let out a deep sigh. Luv-Luv sat in the car, eagerly waiting on her best friend to reply.

Inside the apartment building was a different story. The suspicious activity outside, turned into full blown criminal conduct in the hallways. Spanish Fly stood in front of an apartment door on the second floor in the filthy hallway where crime elevated. He knocked on the door and then couldn't help himself from glancing over in the dark smelly corner to his left because of the gurgling sound and soft moans of pleasure in the atmosphere. When he looked though by no means was it a pleasant sight. Under no circumstances. Spanish Fly watched the dirty homeless old man holding a glass crack pipe between his lips like a cigarette, holding his head, rolling his yellow eyes looking very pleased with his soiled pants down on the floor receiving a night cap in the middle of the day. By young strung out beautiful girl playing offense on her knees so she could score a bag of defense.

"Damn old man gone 'head and do ya thang then," Spanish Fly said laughing to himself, then he lifted the green champagne bottle to his lips, shaking his head in disbelief as he knocked on the door again.

"Aye! Aye! open the door!" Spanish Fly yelled impatiently.

Then he saw, while waiting for someone to open the door and acknowledge his presence. A teenage white boy huddled in a small group of misfits subduing his right arm with a dirty white shoestring and proceeded to do his own thing. The teenage boy penetrated his bluish greenish bulging vein with an old used syringe and injected himself with the controlled substance, bringing forth a warm tingling sensation and calmness over his body before it was nap time. Spanish Fly could tell the stuff was potent because the little white boy was on the verge of curling up like a newborn baby in the fetal position. Not for one second did Spanish Fly have a Sympathetic bone in his body for the young boy getting sleepy while sitting with his misfit group of addict friends. It was a reason why they all were where they were at in life and Spanish Fly believed that deeply as he took another drink to help him think. He felt no remorse for the unfortunate people in the hallway. They all were only collateral damage in something bigger than them and that something was called, economic warfare. These were the broken souls in which he built his success from their empty pockets. They misfortunes were just penalties of wrong decision making.

Spanish Fly had seen enough. He was about to know on the door again but to his surprise is swung open.

"Quit beating on my mothafuckin' door like the cops. Oh shit! I didn't know it was you Spanish Fly. My bad, my bad. Huh, I thought you'd be, um never mind. My dude you hot right now. The hottest nigga in town. C'mon," Profit said ushering Spanish Fly into the crowded apartment. Profit wore a green ostrich skin baseball hat with the alligator brim tilted high on his head and a black hoody. He examined Spanish Fly's condition and snickered.

"Yeah, yeah, c'mon in. So, I guess you here for the rest of that lil' money I owe you, huh?" he asked Spanish Fly, squinting his eyes. The door had just closed behind them when there was another knock. Profit and Spanish Fly stopped and looked at each other. "Awww, don't worry about it. I'll have one of the guys get it," Profit told him flashing a despising smile.

Spanish glanced back at the door, then cut his glossy eyes back at Profit, putting the champagne bottle to his lips and turning it up. Profit put his arm around Spanish Fly's shoulder. "C'mon" he said. They began to walk as the knocking continued. They entered the living room, and it was four savagely looking characters dressed in the same clothes as Profit, satisfying their addiction with drugs and booze. "Aye, aye one of y'all grab the door and handle that, while me and the big homie go in the back and take care of some unfinished business," Profit instructed his company.

Out of the four men, a short ruthless looking man got up to go answer the door. Profit continued to lead Spanish Fly through the huge apartment. Maybe the drink was starting to take a toll on him, or it could have been the strong aroma of fresh poultry that embodied the apartment making him lightheaded.

As they were walking, Spanish Fly was taking into account, business seemed to be doing pretty good in the hood. He witnessed loyal clientele making two, three and four purchases at a time and then speeding out with their big buys. His eyes watched money being exchanged and tallied. Maybe it was the alcohol once again, but his thoughts began to race, if what he was seeing was real, then what was the real deal with Profit? Something definitely was foxy. Why was Profit making him have to wait on his money? Spanish Fly's dirtbag antennas began to rise on his head as he continued to be led in the kitchen. Once they entered the kitchen, Spanish Fly noticed chicken everywhere. That's why it was smelling like fresh poultry throughout the apartment.

He saw an older attractive coffee skinned lady who looked to be in her early fifties, getting her chef game on. She was standing at the stove twerking and her wrist over there huge silver pots cooking birds. She wasn't by herself either. There was a person at the counter battering the raw chicken preparing it to be cooked, then he saw the cooked chicken cooling off on paper towels sitting on glass plates waiting to be chopped up and distributed. He watched another person sitting at the kitchen table making preparations to make a mill. Spanish was becoming upset with what he was seeing.

"Can you explain to my why it's been takin so long to get my money? You have me sitting around waiting on you and shit. Talkin' about, hold on. Shit ain't right. Far as I see shit's good. You making deliveries like the mail man, and you got me on hold? So, what's up with my money Profit?" Spanish Fly asked him a very logical and important question. As he tipped up the champagne bottle to wet his whistle, Profit took his arm from around Spanish Fly's shoulder and stepped back giving him some distance.

"Whoa, Whoa, wait a mothafuckin' minute. Don't be coming at me like that Spanish Fly man. You sitting here puffin out your chest and talkin' slick about some chump change nigga. You need to be worried about Popcorn out here on ya ass, instead of this little case you seating me about," Profit warned him.

Everybody in the kitchen busted out in laughter, but not once stopped with manufacturing. Profit adjusted his hat on his head, then dug in his front pants pocket and pulled out $5500.00 wrapped in three thick rubber bands.

"Huh nigga take this lil' shit. Naw, Naw, you know what? Fuck that. Nigga ya beat, you ain't getting nothin'. Get the fuck out of here before I—"

Profit was hit but he caught himself. Spanish Fly gave him a look of confusion as he stood there to see if Profit was for real.

Everybody in the kitchen stopped laughing and was silent as a mime on the grind.

"Nigga I'm what?" Spanish Fly questioned Profit with his face frowned up mugging the man tryin to set the champagne bottle down. His motor skill was discombobulated because it was entirely too late for that. Before he knew what happened, Profit had cocked back and socked Spanish Fly in the mouth. Sending the champagne bottle through the air and Spanish Fly across the kitchen table, knocking it over, making the product and money spiral in the air. The master chef at the burning stove knocked over the silver pots and the two people who was helping screamed trying to get out of the way of the confrontation. Profit fixed his hat on his head and walked around the turned over the table. He laughed at Spanish Fly laying there curled up in the corner of the kitchen moaning in pain, covered in cocaine residue and scattered money still falling out of the sky. Profit looked at the serious damage he'd caused.

"I been wanting to fuck you up nigga!" he told Spanish Fly and spit on him. Then Profit broadsided the impaired Spanish Fly with a kick to the abdomen, making him vomit on the floor.

Spanish Fly continued to throw up the contents from within himself on the floor.

Luv was sitting in the white Ford Mustang out in front of the brick two story apartment building, she had just hung up the phone still wondering why Sweety hadn't texted her back yet, but that was soon to change. Her phone beeped letting Luv-Luv know she had a new text message in her inbox. When she saw it was Sweety's number, a smile came across her face.

"Thank God, about time girlfriend," she said, then Luv-Luv began to read the message aloud to herself.

"Luv-Luv I forgive you. It's over with for me and I want it to be over with for you, okay? Are you still with Spanish? Huh? Where y'all at?" Luv-Luv exhaled feeling relief.

She was overjoyed knowing her best friend was in a safe place and no longer angry with her anymore. She hurried in testing Sweety back.

Girl right now we at this building picking up some money and then we about to run to the projects real quick and pick up some more money. Then we leaving town too. Luv-Luv typed but she had to keep looking up from the phone.

Between reading and sending text messages, she kept looking out the car window to see people quickly leaving out the apartment building. She begin to sense something wasn't right as if there was danger lurking. Luv-Luv clinched the pink .380 sitting in her lap just in case something shady was about to take place.

Some people just don't know how to quit when they're ahead. Profit was about to continue to play soccer with Spanish Fly until his eyes instinctively saw Spanish Fly advertising the gun metal and wood grain .357 revolver in return for all the disrespect he was receiving. Bah! The thunderous gun blast from the floor had the laughing spectators plowing over each other not trying to catch a heat stroke.

"All nah bitch don't stop kicking me now," Spanish Fly said from down on the floor squeezing the trigger again.

Bah! Profit had a trail of smoke coming from his shoes looking real impressive trying to get up out the kitchen. Spanish Fly jumped to his feet and gave chase trying to give Profit a spiritual uplifting. He was really wanting Profit to see his point of view on this disrespectful matter. When the guns are drawn and shot rang out, tough guys always have a tendency to respond in a sensitive nature.

"Aahhh! C'mon man don't shoot em!" Profit was frantically screaming out as he weaved through the apartment trying to find the nearest exit.

When he found it, Profit darted out the door into the hallway. Bah! The third gunshot grazed Profit's shoulder, but that was all the leverage he needed to haul ass. His hat flew off his head, while at the same time he was flying out the way of bullets. Moving at a fast pace and not paying attention to where he was running, Profit tripped over a white boy taking his afternoon nap on the stairs and fell down a flight of stairs. Spanish Fly was on one, running down the stairs right behind him.

Luv Luv saw more scared looking people ducking and dodging, running out the building trying to get out of harm's way.

"C'mon baby, what is you doing in there?" Luv-Luv said to herself, not knowing, she was about to see exactly what was going on.

Bah! -Click-Click. Spanish Fly had run out of ammunition after giving Profit a gut check. Click-Click. Luv-Luv jumped out the car.

"C'mon baby! C'mon, get in the car!" she yelled over the car roof.

Spanish Fly kneeled down and rummaged through Profit's pockets removing everything in them. Profit balled up gripping his bleeding stomach whining like a toddler with a tummy ache.

"Ow, ohh!" he cried with alligator tears falling from his eyes.

"Shut up nigga, don't nobody wanna hear that shit!" Spanish Fly yelled at him while he was tugging and ripping pockets off the critically injured man's pants.

"What the fuck baby, c'mon, get in the car! Luv-Luv continued to yell out trying to get his attention. Spanish Fly took everything off the man and stood up. Then he looked around and ran to the car. Luv-Luv got into the car at the same time he did and closed the door.

"Drive this mothafucka girl," he ordered her as he empty out the gun so he could reload it. She looked at him breathing heavy and pulled off.

"Baby! Baby? Spanish is you okay?" she asked nervously. He reached over and held her hand.

"Yeah I'm cool. Go to the projects so I can holla at Small-Time and get the rest of my money out here," he told her as he continued to load his pistol.

CHAPTER 21

The first rumble of thunder in the cloudy sky over the concrete jungle should have been a clear indication that trouble was around the corner and rainfall was ahead but this game wasn't getting rained out. The little player spoke with certainty.

"Right, right! I hear you and everything, but peep this my dude, you can't find balls like what I got nowhere else but here, so ain't no deals," Small-Time said.

Small-Time was throwing his sales pitch from the pitcher's mound on the devil's playground, playing hardball. He wanted to let the begging customer know, in this game, there was no free base. Small-Time couldn't afford any handouts or discounts. He wasn't discouraging his customer from making a purchase, but every player had to pay in some kind of way. From the murder out there a couple of days ago, everything had changed. Nothing was the same.

The police had stake outs at the Noware Housing Projects every hour on the hour making sure things were official like a referee whistle. They would occasionally jump out their blue and white squad car, rounding up businessmen and asking for their identification, while making cross-references about what mysteriously happened to Bamboo on live camera. Trying to get someone to piggyback off their inquiries to come up with new information on the situation. Small-Time with his criminal association had a street affiliated associates degree and understood well how the good guys applied pressure to get just about anyone to give them a full lecture on any new developments in the school of hard knocks. Bamboo was a done deal and wasn't nobody out there going to squeal, so everything the police were doing altogether had no arithmetic meaning because it wasn't going to add up correctly. That business with Bamboo was over, soon as he and the esteemed medical team left the crime scene in their emergency vehicle with the flashing red and blue lights in the night, business went back to usual, and the usual suspects were let go to make their dough.

The begging customer decided to become a paying customer and Small-Time began to wrap up the deal with a little advice.

"Huh, take this shit and move around. Next time, man don't be taking all day. I keep tellin' y'all Mothafuckas. The Crown Vic is out here ridin' around laying niggas down. Awe Fuck! See what I'm saying. Don't nobody move. There they go. Shit, shit, they coming down this way," Small-Time said, mad as hell.

Small-Time had been warning everybody about the hot conditions in the projects but didn't nobody care to listen. So as the police hit the corner with the quickness, Small-Time and everybody else was stuck in a sly position, wishing the police would just keep riding through or he and everybody was going to have to do what they had to do. The car slowly approached them with the window rolled down.

"You look nervous. Don't worry Small-Time we don't want you right now. You can relax and sell your stuff. We're looking for your boss Spanish Fly." The crew cut detective wearing dark sunglasses and his partner sitting in the passenger seat yelled out the window of the extremely clean Ford Crown Victoria, shedding some light on the little guy in front of his customer and co-workers. Then the detective quickly spun the steering will to do a U-turn. The car kept going, but Small-Time could still hear the cops laughing as they slowly drove off as he was left viewing the fresh graffiti of burnt tire marks in the middle of the street. Then his little eyes saw the detective on the passenger side talking into his walkie talkie.

Everything was hurting him as he laid in bed sick and tired of hearing the non-stop arguing, yelling, and fighting coming from Small-Time and his associates right outside of his bedroom window. The chastised convict felt it was time to begin his rehabilitation process today. He was becoming light as a feather. The convict was fed up with being fed through a straw but there was nothing he could do. It would be a few months before he could chew food on his own. Left alone, he had sufficient time to think. One thing about the healing process, you inherit a sense of humility. You start thinking inwardly about the quality of life and characteristic behaviors you need to change, to keep you from ever having to suffer prolific pain again. Acts of aggression become gestures of submission. Words of profanity turns into verbal expressions of politeness. You go from hostility to participating in total honest principles. To sum it all up, you basically go from foxy business to minding your own business.

The ten-pound bag of ice, being broke down over a seventy-two-hour span and constantly being applied to the affected areas made the swelling in his head go down. He climbed out of the bed so he could get dressed. His body was sore.

"Mmmm," he groaned wiping slob from his mouth.

He limped to the bathroom and looked in the mirror hanging over the sing and gasped at seeing the pink wounds. The intense pistol whipping he endured had forever altered his glamour. The convict's facial appearance appeared to be permanently disgraced. The man almost collapsed when he saw how abnormal his reflection appeared. The deep, wide, pink gashes engraved across his face being held together by staples were a clear representation of Popcorn. The convict was unidentifiable, he couldn't even recognize himself. His head was now irregular, and his jaw structure had been remodified. Not to mention once again, all the staples across his head and face trying their best to mend the serious damage that was caused. He became emotionally ruined and tears of regret fell from his eyes. Unforgettable flashes of violent images and sounds played back in his mind.

"Huh, shut the fuck up. Huh who tha fuck you talkin to nigga?" The sound of Popcorn's voice haunted him. He still could see the heavy gun being swung across his face as he remembered the warm taste of blood in his mouth, while he was being talked to about his mannerisms.

"Who-can't-sell-what-right-here-nigga?!" He still could hear the proclamation points of Popcorn's speech clear as day, but that.

"I bet ya pussy ass watch who the fuck you talkin' to next time, I betcha." The convict even remembered the wager Popcorn placed on him.

At the shameful memories, he went to wipe the tears from his face, but like his feelings, it hurt because of the pain.

"Mmm," he winced at the attempt.

The convict had seen enough of his disfigured outward appearance. In anger he gently put his clothes on with payback in mind. Then when he was through, he had just one more thing to do. The convict limped to his dresser and opened the bottom dresser drawer. He lifted a neatly set of folded t-shirts and grabbed a black 9mm pistol, checking the magazine, making sure his ammunition was well intact before tucking it in his blue jeans. The convict now was on the fast track of redemption. He pulled down the black hoodie around his waist, concealing the gun and walked out of his bedroom to see his mother sitting in the small kitchen, in her housecoat. She sat at the kitchen table humming her favorite gospel song. Worshipping the lord as she separated her son's pills. Bless her troubled heart. The sanctified woman was concentrating on making sure his meds didn't get mixed up. She never noticed the abomination standing in the doorway of the kitchen, until she accidently dropped one of the pills on the floor next to his shoe.

"Ohh! Jesus!" she frantically screamed at the sight of him. Was it his unannounced presence or his disfigured appearance that almost startled her to death?

"Whoo! Child where did you come from. You can't be sneaking up on me like that. I didn't know you got out of bed," she said with her hand placed on her chest, trying to catch her breath and pretend that his appearance hadn't scared her.

Then him being fully dressed got her full attention.

"Now where do you think you finna go? And watcha thing you finna do? You can't leave out this house hurt like that," she told him as her worry set in and her heartbeat went into overdrive.

It was entirely too dangerous outside her apartment door to just let him go.

"Baby, I was just getting ready to fix you something to eat so you can take your medicine on time like the doctor said. Now gone back in ya room, take them clothes off and get back in bed. If you need something from the store, I'll get it for you. Now please listen to what I said and lay back down in your bed and finish healing up child," said his mother.

His mother nervously pleaded with him as she stood up from the table, hoping he would listen to common sense. When you've been beaten senseless the only thing that makes sense is to knock the sense out of the person's head, who came up with the thought of hurting you.

"Un, nnn, mmm." Saliva hung from his mouth as he tried to spit out what he wanted to say but he couldn't because the wires in his jaw was a communication barrier.

His mother focused her eyes on him, trying her best to catch what he was saying, but they weren't speaking the same language.

"Mmm-mmm, nnn," the convict mumbled still unable to be understood.

Whether she understood him or not, one thing was for certain, his mother could see in his red busted, blood vessel eyes, he was determined to go outside today and not tomorrow or any other days down the line. She dropped her head in grief.

"Since you were a child, I have always disliked that look in your eyes. It only means trouble. It is the same look you have every single time you go to prison, every single time. Do you hear me? Wherever your about to go, I know I can't stop you. I can't take it anymore. I have to give you to God. So, wherever you're going I pray you come back safe, if you're blessed to come back at all," his mother told him as she turned her back on him. It was out of her hands now. She was leaving him in the hands of the lord and walked in her room shaking her head while humming the gospel song like before, then she closed her bedroom door behind her. He checked his waistline, adjusting his gun before heading out the door to go play in the devil's playground.

"Ooh! Shit y'all. Look who finally came out the crib. It's baby mouth!" yelled Small-Time.

Small-Time loudly announced the convict's new and unwanted nickname to everybody out there standing around with a shocked look on their face. As soon as he stepped foot out the door it was on the convict pulled his hood over his irregular head and started stepping through the laughing crowd standing in front of his mother's home. The convict stopped and listened to all the laughter being brought forth at his expense. He clinched his pistol wanting to drop the little comedian with a leg shot, to stop the stand-up comedy show, but now wasn't the time.

"Aww nah, what you stopping for? You ain't on shit, you don't want no problems. Don't make me go get Popcorn out here. He just left not too long ago asking me was you straight. I'm just saying, you straight, huh?" Small-Time was asking him a simple question.

The convict decided at that moment it was best to just keep walking. There was going to be a day soon to come, something bad was going to happen to this little kid. The convict kept his cool and continued to go on about his way.

"Yeah that's what I thought. You better keep it moving. Yeah keep it moving right along," Small-Time pressed on with taunting the man until he crossed the street.

"Punk Mothafucka!" he yelled at the convict. As the man walked through the gangway of the two burnt vacant buildings disappearing.

"Damn that nigga looked real fucked up Small-Time. He don't even look the same," one of Small-Time' guys said, giving an acute depiction of what he just saw.

They all laughed it off and got back on point. The projects natural produced propane to spread heat in the streets. The new flame named Lil' Mitch was hot and crispy. The slim blow torch dressed dapper looking spiffy with his eyes, low feeling nifty, walking through the land of drama on his way to the studio to finesse the mic for commas. He stopped for a hot second to rap with Small-Time and promote his dope. Lil' Mitch kept pure smoke and had just finished manufacturing a new song last night. He slid through the hood, wanting to see if the elements were right before he laid out the invite for other lyrical chemists to put the mix on it, making it a bomb. He walked up and shook hands with everybody and them posted up on the scene.

"What's up? What's up with y'all. I ain't got a lotta time right now to chill. They been calling me all day to get in the lab and spas out but check this out. I been thinking 'bout shooting my next music video out here, fuckin' around with y'all. What's up Small-Time? You wit it? I got this new song I just finished and on my kids! Boy it's raw! Aye, Aye, I'm finna scorch y'all ears real quick."

The whole city dark and shit.

All these guns draw like its art and shit.

Don't give em lighter fluid cuz the sparkin' shit.

They probably shoot and hit the baby at the park and shit.

And when it's nighttime

I keep a black grizzly I'ma

Let 'em hold fifty man. I'm tellin' you what nigga in

His right mind gone run up on this hem? I'ma

Get off out tha window got his family on the

Grilly like he might die.

No Killa don't push me.

Got no feelins for puss

Lotta snitching man tell 'em.

Don't book me/Molly wit' the Remy ain't no tellin' where it took me.

His magma flow was cut off by the rough crowd going up in amazement, giving him their approval.

"Whoa, whoa, aw man hold up man, that's real smoke Lil' Mitch. Hell, yeah you gotta shoot the video out here in the jets wit' us," Small -Time told him and at the same time watching a white Ford Mustang quickly gallop around the corner coming into the projects running good.

It came roaring down the street catching everybody's attention as it came to a stop in the parking lot.

"Small-Time, who is that?" Lil' Mitch asked reaching around his waist just in case he had to put a large hole in someone's face.

Small-Time like everyone else out there watched the car with caution.

"Man, Lil' Mitch you asking me? Shit I should be asking you, on the real I don't know who tha fuck that is," he responded back.

Then he heard the sound of a lot of guns being cocked and getting ready to explode.

"Whoa y'all hold on before y'all do that, A'ight?" Small-Time said, holding his hand up, hoping didn't nobody shoot the car up before they could see who it was.

<h1 style="text-align:center">CHAPTER 22</h1>

Like the black plague, death in the black community had become an epidemic which seemed to spread rapidly with no known cure insight. Nevertheless, there was no cooperation between the citizens and law enforcement. The police had to do some real work to fight crime by beefing up manpower to patrol the streets.

"Okay. Okay white sports car period now I think we might be getting somewhere. Who do we have here?" the undercover officer said in a questioning manner, placing a piece of chewing gum in his mouth trying to get a good look at the white Ford Mustang pulling into the parking lot of the Noware Housing Projects.

They used hot coffee for libation and binoculars for surveillance. As the two detectives sat a few blocks down the street away from the hottest housing projects in the whole city. They went over clues.

"So Spanish Fly or Popcorn? Which one of them you think clip the girl from the beauty store?" the skinny detective sitting in the passenger seat asked his partner while taking a sip of coffee from his cup.

The crew cut detective sitting in the driver seat chewed his gum and continue to look through his binoculars. He kept his eyes on the prize which was the white Ford Mustang sitting in the parking lot and Small-Time standing out there with the other overqualified murder suspects.

"Let me tell you something partner I don't have to think who killed that girl because I already know exactly who it was that murdered her period, it was that crazy fucker Popcorn who left her dead covered in money. Are you listening? Now follow me on this one for a second you hear. The girl was working at the beauty supply store when a man walks in and started shooting the place up, but she doesn't tell us anything. No, why can't she give us not one single description of the triggerman? I'll tell you why, she's involved somehow. I don't know how just yet, but I know she was. Okay are you still with me on this one partner?" the crew cut detective asked.

He sat the binoculars on the dashboard and tested the temperature of his coffee. Getting himself a little taste of Columbia's finest, and then went on.

"Ahh yeah, yeah that's good stuff. Now where was I, oh, okay. The elderly man killed yesterday in the intersection wasn't some good old Samaritan who retired from a factory after forty laborious years on the job. No, no, no. That old man was feared. He was a well-known and well-respected criminal, who never talked much because of a missing tongue that was cut out of his mouth by two very dangerous men named Bino and Scat, which, neither is no longer living. Oh yes, I almost forgot, the old man just so happens to be Popcorn's uncle. Now, the people witnessing that shooting described a man fitting Spanish Fly's description and leaving the murder scene in a white Chrysler Town & Country minivan. Am I right? Okay, this morning the young girl, Detective Whitaker called Sweety is found slumped over the seat in a White Chrysler Town & Country minivan, dead with $3,000.00 scattered over her body. The same white minivan our shooter was driving. Are the dots starting to connect for you partner? She was paid $3,000.00 to keep silent and now she's permanently quiet. The $3,000.00 is what got her killed." The crew cut detective was trying to bring his partner up to speed on his hypothesis.

Instead of knocking on doors trying to come up on new leads the crew cut detective was going off another one of his hunches. Being that the Noware Housing Projects is where Popcorn and Spanish Fly launched their criminal careers. There was a surety that either Popcorn or Spanish Fly or both would show up out there eventually and if in the event they did, it was going to be hard for them to evade the good guys. The evidence written in the middle of the housing project's streets was exceptional proof that at least one of the criminals had already made their presence known today and probably would be back. Every police officer in the city who took an oath to protect and serve, were under strict orders from the police commissioner himself that the birds weren't going to chirp another morning without Spanish Fly and Popcorn being in custody or in a casket. One way or another, they were coming off the streets.

***

Spanish Fly sat in the car of the parking lot already pissed. He became hotter watching Small-Time standing on a different block than where he should have been.

"Why in the fuck is he posted up over here, when he's supposed to be on that other block taking care of business?" Spanish Fly asked in confusion.

Luv-Luv looked at Spanish Fly and shrugged her shoulders. She couldn't provide a logical explanation for Small-Time's new disposition.

"I don't know Spanish, maybe he's trying to expand," she volunteered reasoning.

"Nah, nah, I ain't trying to hear that. That ain't what it is. This lil' mothafucka just been out here Jimmy Flickin' and bulshittin'. And why he ain't coming to this car? I know damn well his lil' ass see me right here," Spanish Fly said aggravated.

Even though Spanish Fly heard Luv Luv's reassurance, he

took a sip of cognac and took what she said into consideration.

"All I know is I ain't got time for this shit. His lil' ass better come ova here and bring my money," Spanish Fly said while letting the tinted passenger window roll down so Small-Time would recognize him.

Small-Time and his compadres all stood there watching the white car clutching their pistols as the passenger window dropped.

"Aw shit Small-Time, that's ya big homie Spanish Fly in that car. Aye look you cool, that's ya mans. Check this out, I'm finna go to the studio and lay these tracks. I'll be back and let you know when we gonna shoot the video," the one named Lil' Mitch said.

He walked off shaking everybody's hand and went to go handle his business. Small-Time looked Spanish Fly in the eyes like a square sitting in the car and didn't move. That's when the first raindrop fell from the heavens. A thunderstorm was on its way. Everybody standing around started to move around.

"Damn man it's finna get ready to rain. Aye Small-Time, I'll be back. I'm finna fix me something to eat. I'm hungry as hell. You want me to bring you something back?" one of his other fellow workers asked him.

"Yeah man you do that," Small-Time said still watching Spanish Fly watching him like a hawk.

"Aye hold up, what you finna make? I'm hungry too. I'm finna go with you," another one of Small-Time's concerned fellow workers said as he moved around because of hunger pangs and to get out of the rain. Small-Time, with anger in his eyes looked at all his homies trying to dip out.

"Yeah, you know what? You do just that, A'ight?" Small-Time said to his so-called starving friend.

Then he sat his little eyes back on Spanish Fly, still sitting in the car looking at him, while in the distance the convict crossed the street to enter back into the projects with a bag of ice. It was written on the wall for all to see and was a well-known fact, people don't know how to act when it looked like you were losing in the streets. Everyone seemed to get disrespectful. People treated and talked to you any type of way they felt like, including your own people, especially your own people. It was as if, they felt like you wouldn't do them any harm. This was what foxy business was in Spanish Fly's opinion, when you do not get acknowledged, when Spanish Fly knew for sure Small-Time knew exactly who he was. Spanish Fly had been definitely shown a sign of disrespect from his little worker.

"What this lil' mothafucka think I'm playing games? I'll be right back," Spanish Fly said to Luv-Luv as he got out the vehicle.

Spanish Fly in doing so, opened the cylinder of the .357 snub nose revolver. He spun it around making sure it would sing like the Spinners when and if he needed to start shooting, but decided he'd close it back with anticipation.

"Un-uh, au grand sieriexu. Now wait one damn minute Spanish, I know damn well you ain't about to pull no gun out on that lil' boy, is you? He's only a baby," Luv-Luv asked him.

Spanish Fly pressed the button on the passenger door to roll up the window before he rolled out and rolled on Small-Time.

"Hell nah, what do I look like? I'm finna pop shorty lil' ass if he don't have my cash. He gonna learn at an early age about fuckin with people's money," Spanish Fly corrected Luv-Luv on what was about to take place. He tucked the revolver, opened the door, and jumped out the car.

Meanwhile, the two detectives who sat in the green Crown Victoria, had changed their focus.

"Hey, hey partner tell me you don't see that, right there. The Camaro, the black Camaro sitting up there at the traffic lights in the turning lane. That's going to be my retirement present to myself. Sweet Jesus, just look at it how it moves around corners with such confidence and ease. The pure American muscle underneath the hood of such a beauty just made my adrenaline rush, I tell ya," the crew cut detective said with praise admiring what he believed to be his dream car. But as the car drew nearer, he realized he almost missed his beat.

"Oh shit! Did he just get out the white car!" he yelled, putting the binoculars up to his eyes?

His antennas went up when he realized who the black man was who exited the white car they had been surveil lancing in the parking lot of the projects.

"Wait, wait, is that-and yes, it is. Partner we got one of my friends. Hello, hello, Mr. Spanish Fly," the crew cut detective said with a smile and handed the binoculars over to his partner

"Yep! That's him alright," the other detective responded.

Spanish Fly was feeling the pressure now, he hated to say it but he knew it was the type of pressure that made loyalty deteriorate. His mind was going a hundred miles an hour, thinking, *the ones you teach. Trust can breach. The him or me mentality comes into play and well you know how that plays out.* Even after giving Small-Time the game, Spanish Fly, could tell as he walked up, his little protégé wasn't the same. He could see in the little guy's posture that the kid was and imposter. All the rules and regulation he tried to implement into Small-Time was deleted and Spanish Fly wanted to erase his memory bank if Small-Time's little pockets were bankrupt. Spanish Fly walked up on him as the rain began to fall lightly. Small-Time leaned back against the brick wall of the housing projects looking composed.

"Lil' nigga why tha fuck you ain't come holla at me when you seen me roll the windows down. Oh, so this how we conduct business? And why tha fuck you posted up over here instead of where you should be, huh?" Spanish Fly asked.

Spanish Fly all of a sudden changed his composure and attempted to be reasonable before he let Small-Time have it.

"Man, you asking me all these questions -hold on, hold on,

Aye, yo, yo baby mouth pump yo brakes. Don't come walking through me and my big homie conversation. Nigga you stay right there," Small-Time said authoritatively.

"Boy who tha fuck is you talkin' to like that?" Spanish Fly said in amazement as he turned his head to see who Small-Time was giving orders too like he was tough. The horror at what Spanish Fly saw made him and grimace.

"Whoa! Awe shit! Ugh man," Spanish Fly couldn't help himself from blurting out. Then he looked back at Small-Time with shock and now had even more questions for the little fellow.

"Un-uh, man. What tha fuck happened to buddy?" he asked Small-Time as though the disfigured convict wasn't standing there and couldn't hear them talking.

The convict didn't move an aching muscle only because he had a good memory of what took place last time, he rudely interrupted one of Small-Time's conversations. He just waited in the rain holding on to the ten pound bag of ice, but now his mind was made up, he had no questions in his mind. He was going to beat the shit out of the little kid when the time was right. Small-Time lifted his eyebrows and shook his head.

"Popcorn my boi. Popcorn, that's what happened to him," Small-Time said in a cool and calm voice.

Spanish Fly looked back at the aftermath displayed on the disfigured convict's face and got the chills. Damn, he whispered to himself. Then he looked around the projects to make sure there wasn't a soul outside but them.

"Fuck this shit," he said and got back to business .

"So Popcorn did that huh, so tell me what else did Popcorn come out here and do? You better not say he took my money," Spanish Fly said to Small-Time.

Small-Time looked around and spit on the ground.

"You asking me all these questions man and every answer is gonna end with Popcorn," Small-Time told him. Spanish Fly looked at the kid disturbed.

"Lil' nigga, I'ma ask you one more time where my money and you betta not—" The anger wouldn't allow Spanish Fly to finish the question.

Small-Time kept his cool and positioned his right foot up against the brick wall, then looked Spanish Fly dead in the eyes and gave his answer.

"Popcorn got it," Small-Time said.

Spanish Fly looked back at the disfigured convict once again and walked up on the still, calm cool and collective Small-Time.

"Mothafucka!" he said gritting his teeth and pulled out the snub nose .357 and shoved it into Small-Time's stomach getting ready to put the kid back in a diaper.

"Aaah! Man, what I do?" Small-Time screamed out frantically raising his hands up in surrender, towards the sky. The clouds up above crashed making a thunderous noise. The convict tried to smile at what he was seeing but couldn't, so he just watched with pleasure.

While up the road, sat the two detectives viewed all the criminal activities from a safe distance.

"Oh! Oh! Jesus did he just pull a gun on the kid? Call for back up, call for back up right now, he's about to shoot the kid," said the skinny detective sitting in the passenger seat of the green Crown Victoria. The crew cut detective quickly took the binoculars back from his honorable partner to have a look see of his own and laughed.

"Whoa, uh, hold on there before you go calling the calvary. You don't know this kid. I'm telling you now. You don't have to worry about the little guy, believe me. He's a piece of work. I hope I'm long gone before he's a grown man. I tell ya that much," he told the detective sitting in the passenger seat. The skinny detective's heart was pumping fast, and his blood was rushing through his veins, watching what was going on.

"Well right now it doesn't look like he's going to make it to see tomorrow. Now call for back up," he cried.

"Just watch what I tell ya, this lil' guy stays with a gimmick," the crew cut detective reassured his nervous partner as he continued to peer through the binoculars at the hostile situation, amused.

Trying not to lose his life in the rain, Small-Time stood up against the brick wall with his hands high not wanting to die.

"C'mon Spanish Fly, this ain't for us. What I look like getting down on you? Yeah, I do what I gotta do out here, but you, you awe nah, anybody but you man. I ain't bullshitting wit' you. Popcorn took all the mothafuckin' money. Ya hear me? Look at the street. You see them tire marks? He just been through here a while ago asking had I seen you. I told him nope. Then he started going crazy and shit," Small-Time said, trying to look convincing, then he added a little bit more sauce to his story so it would be believable.

"Man! I'm telling you, look at the street and big dudes face," Small-Time said pointing to the street and the disfigured convict standing behind Spanish Fly trying to plead for his young life.

"Oh, he did, huh?" Spanish Fly questioned Small-Time's sincerity. Then Spanish Fly took the initiative to start roughly digging through Small-Time's healthy pockets, making the kid sick and his little pants almost fall to the ground.

"Oh, look at this. Huh, huh? What the fuck is this? Huh, what's all of this? Lil' mothafucka, you just lied and told me Popcorn took everything but ya mothafuckin' pockets on full," Spanish Fly said as he was removing thousands of dollars.

"Ah nah, wait! Wait!" Small-Time contested. Poor little Small-Time was frantic, he was on pins and needles. His future from this point on looked bleak. It seemed like Spanish Fly would never stop pulling money out of his pockets.

"Huh, mothafucka, Popcorn took everything. Yeah, I see. Un-huh Popcorn took everything, huh?" Spanish Fly kept talking as he kept pulling money from everywhere and in anger cocked back the hammer on the .357 snub nose revolver. Small-Time's little intestines were trembling where the gun touched the tender spot of his stomach. At gunpoint it was clear that the scam was over. The time had come for the little schemer to expose his hand.

"A'ight! A'ight! He told me to tell you—" Small-Time's confession was shot short.

"Mmm!!!" the disfigured convict tried to yell out in pain through the wires in his mouth. The ten pound bag of ice and the black 9mm all fell to the ground at the same time.

"Mmm-Naa!" the convict continued screaming in pain, while urine saturated the front of his pants, and he gripped his bloody buttocks.

"Mmm." Spanish Fly and Small-Time paused from what they were doing. They both panicked, looking down on the ground at the bleeding convict groping in pain. That's when they realized he had been critically wounded by a gunshot.

"How tha fuck he get shot? I didn't hear nothing," Small-Time said, looking bewildered. Then Spanish Fly and Small-Time started recognizing the familiar sound of bullets traveling through the air, striking windows, making them shatter.

"Ahh!" Small-Time yelled not knowing what was happening. Bullets were ricocheting off walls and hitting cars. They saw bullet holes mysteriously appearing out of nowhere. It was design by chance giving Spanish Fly the opportunity to glance up at the right time to keep from dying. When Spanish Fly got wind, the shots were being aimed directly at him, it was time to make physical efforts to live. He saw Popcorn dressed in green army fatigues and tan boots running and gunning in his direction, squeezing the trigger of a Mac II specially equipped with the silencer trying to kill the animosity between them. He had to do the limbo trying to get out of the limbo he was currently in.

"Ahh shit mothafucka!" Spanish Fly yelled, grabbing Small-Time using him as a human shield. Bah`Bah! The .357 had a violent outburst trying to put Popcorn horizontal in the back of a hearse. Spanish Fly ran with screaming kid in front of him.

"Mothafucka." He was cussing and busting while back pedaling towards the parking lot.

Talking on the phone Luv-Luv wasn't paying any attention to the attempt murder going on outside the car. That quickly changed though, when the passenger and driver windows shattered, and broken glass fell in her lap from a stray shot, or was it? "Aah! Aah!" she screamed dropping the phone as bullets flew passed her face. She was hearing and feeling the car being struck by even more bullets. There was no need for second guessing. It clearly seemed as if the bullets were meant for her.

"Ahh! Ahh! Ahh!" she kept screaming, looking at Spanish Fly and Popcorn shooting at each other in the middle of the projects, running towards the car she occupied, in conjunction with the police entering the projects behind them at the same time. Luv-Luv didn't know what to do.

Her gun was in her purse and her options were few. It was either death, jail, or bail. She made a split decision when she took her foot and stomped on the gas pedal. The tires started screeching as rubber peeled off onto the street. As she peeled out in the white Ford Mustang, fishtailing out of the Noware Housing Projects parking lot without Spanish Fly in the passenger seat or window. The game was deep.

Trying not to lose his head, heading towards the car, Spanish Fly was concentrating on hitting his target and staying alive. He could see a blue and white police car quickly coming down the street and Luv-Luv speeding sideways out the parking lot in the corner of his eye. He kept pulling the trigger. Bah!

"No! No! No! where the fuck is, she going?" he said in desperation.

She still had love for him, but Luv-Luv had to follow the number one cardinal rule in the book of life. For her it was self-preservation before visitation and cremation with no hesitation. Luv-Luv ducked behind the steering wheel of the sport car pulling a maneuver to get out of harm's way. She kept flinching still being able to hear gunshots ringing out in the distance. Not knowing if it was meant for her, she continued to peek over the dashboard as she turned the corner getting away with her life. Bah! Bah! Click! Click. His gun was empty, and Popcorn was gone. Spanish Fly pushed Small-Time down to the ground and ran straight into the hood of the police car. He threw the gun down and put his hands in the air. The police officer immediately jumped out of the squad car with his gun drawn.

"Motherfucker, don't you move!" Spanish Fly kept his hands up and kept looking around trying to see which way Popcorn slipped to.

"Put your hands on the hood of the car!" the police officer commanded. Spanish Fly did exactly what he said. He definitely wasn't trying to get fatally shot by a trigger-happy cop, looking for another notch on his gun handle. Small-Time got up and broke out. Spanish Fly with his hands on the car watched the little boy vanish into the projects.

"Didn't I tell ya don't worry about the kid. Huh? Didn't I tell ya? That was fucking unbelievable. That kid is something else. He's gonna be a real bad ass when he gets older. Lucky for Spanish Fly that squad car showed up when it did. Alright partner now you can call for back up." The crew cut detective gave his partner the okay to call for assistance. After they watched the gun show from the green Crown Victoria down the street. The storm seemed to pass on and no one passed away.

"Shots have been fired. I repeat shots have been fired." The skinny detective sitting in the passenger seat made the call finally. While the crew cut detective tickled himself pink over what went down.

"Oh yeah and partner you better radio in some medical assistance too, while you're at it, for the big guy on the ground shot in the ass." The crew cut detective suggested, while they both laughed

CHAPTER 23

It is imperative for the residents of the community to feel a sense of security. Three very nervous news reporters positioned themselves in front of the camera men trying to keep the microphones in their hands from shaking. They were out in the dead of night being paid to shine some light on the malicious crimes in the projects.

When there's a public outcry to cease the violence, then there's a must for the police to apprehend a subject and put the criminals on public display. The trick of seeing a captured criminal in the public eye is a false translation of public safety. Raw footage flashing across a television screen, of hoodlums in handcuffs in neglected neighborhoods, only hoodwinks the naïve viewer. Look past the criminal, not meaning give the criminal a pass but look deep into the problem at hand.

Like a fly caught in a glass jar a large crowd of people stood outside watching him. Spanish Fly sat handcuffed in the back seat of a blue and white squad car. Far as Spanish Fly was concerned, all the people standing around the projects staring at him could look all they wanted to. He'd rather go to jail than be laying on top of a cold steel autopsy table dead. What really played with his head was this. Why would the woman he loved pull off and leave him to get smoked? Yellow tape with the word 'Shooting' kept the nosy on lookers at bay so they wouldn't infiltrate the crime scene.

The police searching the area wanted every shred of evidence they could find. They wanted to make sure he would be confined to a prison cell for a long time. The police placed yellow triangle tags down to decorate the ground, so they could keep tabs on the amount of shell casings were spent at the cost of life and death.

Small-Time had got out that jam and it was showtime. He no doubt was right back at it again with the cell phone in his hand. Him and his team intervened on the crime scene along with a very large crowd of deliberating spectators standing in suspense to survey the damage done. They wanted to go and tell their friends the story the way they saw fit. Small-Time was tired of looking at Spanish Fly sitting in the back of the police car. He walked through the crowd and over to the area where the handcuffed convict was being lifted on a stretcher. The police found the gun he had laying on the ground next to him when they arrived. He was under arrest, but the police were allowing him to get the proper medical assistance. The paramedics had cut the convict's pants and underwear off. They had him lying on his stomach with his bleeding buttocks hanging out in the neighborhood for all those to see. That had caught the attention of Small-Time's dirt bag antennas and he felt it would catch the attention of his online viewers too. He too his cell phone and went live on social media. Small-Time was giving his online followers a never before seen inside edition on some real mess. He focused the camera on himself with the yellow tape behind him for his background and began to get on with the show.

"Awe man! What tha fuck you mean. It's been goin down out here today. Punk ass Spanish Fly just got caught down bad. He over here right now sitting in the back seat of the police car. Yeah, Yeah, he just had me in a shootout wit' 'em, but I got up outta there when the cops came. I hope he don't mention my name. Ya feel me? I ain't got nothin' to say but naw you feel me. I want everybody to check this nigga out right her though." Then

Small-Time turned the camera onto the critically injured convict being attended to by emergency responders.

"I know y'all remember him, uh, hold up real quick. Wait, wait, let me get a close up for y'all," Small-Time said zooming in the focus on the camera phone.

"Can you see him now? Wait, okay, yeah, that's it. Him lying on the stretcher with is black ass hanging out." Laughing hysterically while he continued.

"Now y'all remember my dude. Yep he the nigga got all his teeth knocked out his mouth, the other day. I call him baby mouth." He couldn't resist humiliating him, again.

"Yep mothafuckin' baby mouth, that's his new name. The ambulance people takin' him to the hospital right now because he just got shot in the ass, two times. I'm telling y'all it was funny as hell though." Small-Time almost fell to his knees with laughter, giving his viewers a grade A performance.

Being discreet Popcorn smoothly walked across the street towards the action. He had quickly changed clothes and came back to a cluttered project. His work brought the whole city out. He snuck in the projects with his dark colored hood on and just like every other criminal that comes back to the scene of the crime, he stood around blending into the night and the crowd. Popcorn's cold calculated red eyes glimmered through the chaotic crowd. He watched a spooked Spanish Fly sitting in the back of a squad car looking out of the windows. Popcorn kept his head down trying not to be recognized. He still concealed and carried the Mac II with the silencer hanging from a shoestring over his shoulder underneath the dark colored hoodie. He continued to slowly step and stop through people. He could hear the liars and skeptics chit-chatting about what took place out there and why Spanish Fly was in the police car.

"I can't stand y'all mothafuckas. Y'all don't know shit," Popcorn angrily mumbled to himself wanting to shoot some of them standing around, but he cancelled that thought and kept moving closer to his target in the police car.

The police like the crowd of onlookers were too busy chit chatting and trying to look good for the news cameras to notice that death was standing in their midst. Popcorn had eased his way through the rigmarole and was standing right at the yellow tape looking directly at a paranoid Spanish Fly in the face. It amused Popcorn watching Spanish Fly's head rotate like an owl, trying to see where he was at. Popcorn stood there and cocked the machine gun just waiting for his childhood friend to lay eyes on him before he laid Spanish Fly to rest. At that very moment Popcorn had a thought entered his mind.

"All this for nothing," he said to himself under his breath and that's when Spanish Fly's eyes grew wide at the sight of him.

Popcorn spit over the yellow tape onto the ground and nodded his head towards Spanish Fly, letting Spanish Fly know that he brought this on himself. Spanish Fly's heart was pounding hard and fast he became hysterical in the back seat of the police car. He was kicking and throwing himself around, looking like he was yelling for the police, who was at the time, too busy collecting evidence against him to help him. The crowd became aroused watching Spanish Fly carrying on in the back seat. This played out perfectly for Popcorn. The noise factor and all. Popcorn slightly lifted up his dark colored hoodie so Spanish Fly could see the silencer on the Mac II. To the crowd of onlookers Spanish Fly was going crazy in the back seat of the police car.

"What's wrong with him? He act like he finna die back there or something." A beautiful dark-skinned woman told another spectator standing to her side witnessing the same thing she was seeing. Popcorn dropped his head to the ground.

"My uncle? Nigga," he whispered, then he lifted his head and the Mac II at the same time. He looked at Spanish Fly for the last time and had a disregard for life.

Popcorn pulled the trigger making the machine gun whistle at the police car tearing Spanish Fly apart. Popcorn was letting hot lead rapidly descend up Spanish Fly, while he helplessly sat in the back seat subdued in handcuffs. The crowd went wild at seeing windows busting and the car door being quietly shredded up. Spanish Fly's body jerked around from being twerked with Mac II rounds. The bullets were eating him alive like carnivores. His blood was painting the back seat of the police car red. Popcorn continued to shoot until he felt a gun placed on the back of his head and heard it being cocked to rock his top.

"Ahh, gotcha! Put the fucking gun down Popcorn or I will end your show right fucking now. This is the police, and this is your only warning!" the sneaky crew cut detective yelled his orders in order for Popcorn to live.

Even with a pistol placed to the back of his head, he took pleasure in watching his friend grotesquely, gurgle, coughing up blood struggling for air and dying a slow painful death. Spanish Fly was trying to cling on to what little dear life he still had left. The sound of him struggling for air while his lungs filled up with blood, looking at Popcorn wanting to say something, but couldn't do so because death, creeping in wouldn't allow him to. His lungs were filling up with blood, drowning him while Popcorn and everyone else watched. Popcorn wasn't a person who took heed to warning so he went back to carrying on with what he was doing. Popcorn applied more pressure to his friend, by applying more pressure to the Mac II. Silent shots in the night continued to relentlessly rip Spanish Fly apart in front of everyone.

The bold actions of Popcorn left the crew cut detective no other choice. The detective relinquished three quick shots, Pop-Pop-Pop. Being a civil servant, the crew cut detective pulled the trigger on his service pistol into the back of Popcorn's head. Pink brain matter splattered on the clothes, skin, and in the hair of the nosy spectators. At the sound of gunshots people hit the ground ducking for cover. The paramedics helping the convict, knocked him off the stretcher trying to find some sort of safety from being stretched out. While others ran from the shots, law enforcement employees rushed over to develop a double murder scene. The local news camera men captured the explicit footage of Spanish Fly's head leaned back hanging halfway out the shattered back window with his eyes and mouth wide opened. Then they focused the huge camera on their shoulders down to the ground, where they found Popcorn positioned with his body curled underneath the shot-up police car. He was missing chunks of his face, courtesy of exit wounds. He laid on the ground in a pool of blood still holding on to the Mac II with the silencer.

"You won't be needing that anymore," the crew cut detective said kicking the machine gun out of the dead bloody hand of Popcorn.

"I've been waiting all day for this. I knew you would be back tonight. It was just in your nature, huh? After all you were an apex predator," the crew cut detective kneeled down talking to the faceless Popcorn.

Small-Time ran back over to the car where he'd last seen Spanish Fly. He paused in his tracks with a shocked look on his face at what he saw.

"Whoa! They both dead." In the game ain't no game. Nine times out of ten it'll be one of your friends that will do you in and that, so called girl you loved so much? Well, you know.

CHAPTER 24

etrayal unfortunately wouldn't even scratch the surface of her many talents. Accommodate and accumulate was her distinctive trademark. Exceptionally experience in the field of capital gain, Luv-Luv followed the course set before her. Cut by shattered glass, battered by the ordeal of death and destruction. She knew how to take appropriate measures in obtaining treasures under lock and key. Objectives and obligation both had been met in the rough romantic plot. That would bring forth a desirable outcome. Luv-Luv had been one of his most meaningful weapons in his arsenals of go-getters.

Taken by the attraction of the Atlantic Ocean captured in the black marble wall, Luv-Luv marveled at watching sharks swimming around in the customized fish tank. She removed her shoes placing her beautiful, pedicured feet on the polished hardwood floor. "Is there anything I can get for you? A refreshment perhaps?" she was asked by a pretty petite sandy brown Persian beauty with long black hair and gray hypnotic eyes.

"Um no, I'ma just sit here and wait, okay?" Luv-Luv told the naked Persian maid standing in red stilettos.

"Well alright if there's nothing else, he knows you're here." And then disappeared as quickly as she appeared.

Luv-Luv sat at the glossy oak wood table feeling a sense of

relief. Hard at work and gone for so long, she was back home where she belonged. Under a deep hypnosis, Luv-Luv's green eyes compared to her movements in the streets. To the non-emotional predators in the wall, moving stealthily in water. Her occupation to greatly influence prey out of their pay is how she survives. She blinked and seen a beautiful Native American girl with long hair dressed in a pink lace negligée walking through the home. The girl stopped when she saw Luv-Luv sitting alone at the glossy hardwood table. Then the girl took it upon herself to make a formal introduction. After all, why not? She gave an articulate oral presentation, proving how beneficial she would be to his company which solidified her employment with the Pleasurable Performing Act Incorporated, also known as P.P.A. Inc.

"Hi, I take it you're Luv-Luv. I've heard some amazing stories about you. It's nice to finally meet you, my name is Meow and I want to just say you're a purrty woman." Meow complemented Luv-Luv with the roll of her tongue reminiscent of Eartha Kitt as Cat Woman. Luv-Luv with her green eyes knew the girl was green, but she was a part of the team.

"Well thank you," Luv-Luv told her and went back to admiring the real predators in the black marble wall. The new girl understood the unspoken message and quickly made her exit and left Luv-Luv to her thoughts. Luv-Luv considered how pretty the new girl was but smelled even better. The way the lightly scented fragrance mixed Meow's natural pheromones had Luv-Luv aroused.

"Desire, seduction, temptation bought the big bucks," she said to herself, repeating what she had been taught by Macvicious. She thought about her new friend Sweety she had met on the job. Sweety wouldn't even consider living the lifestyle, but Luv-Luv was going to continue to keep Sweety as her friend. She took her cell phone out and texted Sweety's phone.

"I just wanna know you have you made it there yet? Text

me back okay?" Once finished with the text, she put the cell phone back in her purse with the pink pistol and more valuable assortments. Her heart went back to pumping fast, when her mind played back to the glass shattering and the look Spanish Fly had in his eyes when he was running back to the car, holding the little boy in front of him trying not to get killed. Then she thought about the night Popcorn interrupted her sexual seduction with A-K bullets. Visions from Popcorn walking in the beauty supply sent chills through her body and she could still remember his voice.

Bitch you wanna kill me, huh?

Macvicious gazed over the beautiful tight naked bodies of the Russian twins laying in his soft king-sized bed, bodies misted with sweat and disheveled hair. Never seen in public, they displayed smiles of satisfaction on their beautiful faces. He closed the bedroom door on his foreign affairs and went to see if the local business ventures financially improved. He could see his exotic French Creole mademoiselle sitting at the table of values with her head down.

"Desire, seduction, temptation, lust, brought big bucks," he spoke walking down the hallway to uplift her. Her head rose from the table, smiling at the viewing pleasure of Macvicious. With a walk that rivaled that of Denzel Washington, dressed in pajama bottoms, adorned with jewels on his writs, fingers and chest that caught the light casting prisms on the walls. Without even speaking she was making preparations to give him a warm, wet reception.

"What happened when I was talking to you on the phone earlier? I heard you screaming and shit, then the phone went dead," he asked wanting to know about the disconnection.

"Once again I almost got killed. Them niggas got to shooting at each other again and I don't know what happened because I took off on his ass, but everything went just like you said it would between them," she said standing up from the table and wrapping her arms around his neck, giving him a hug.

"Hmm, I've been missing you, holding on to you feels so good". They sat at the table of values to talk about business.

"Last night after we saw the news, I thought Spanish Fly was going to propose to me." With a giggle she said, "I thought about saying yes, why not, he wasn't going to make it to the wedding anyway." Macvicious laughed with her.

She continued, "But he didn't propose, he was scared of going to jail and leaving me out here broke. That nigga did everything you said he would. Huh, here you go baby a contribution from Spanish Fly and that crazy nigga Popcorn. I have to go to the clinic in the morning and take care of whatever needs to be taken care of so I can get back to work." Placing the valuables from her purse on the table, he smiled at what he saw, but didn't touch anything.

"This is everything right?" he asked, and she answered with a nod. "See the streets is open now. Just found out both of them niggas is outta here. They're gone. You sure this is all the keys to the safe houses and the combinations to all the safes?"

With a laugh he said, "See I told you Spanish Fly and Popcorn's conflict was going to be in my best interest." Luv-Luv's phone began to ring, taking it out her purse she looked at the screen and a smile came over her face. "This is the girl I was telling you about," she said answering the call. "What's up girl? You made it? What time did you get off the bus?" Luv-Luv was so happy to get a call from Sweety that she was talking a mile a minute.

"Sorry, this isn't Sweety, this is Detective Whitaker." Suddenly her smile disappeared and was replaced by distress. The detective continued and said,

"She was murdered this morning and we've just located her cell phone in the pocket of a man who is also deceased. He went by the street name of Popcorn. I would like for you to come down to the station and answer a few questions we still have about Sweety's case—"

She hung up the phone and dropped it on the floor. Tears flowed from her green eyes. Maybe she wasn't exactly the non-emotional predator swimming in the wall, but he was.

"Aye I don't know why you are crying, and I don't care to know, get up and let the maid clean you up," Macvicious said, annoyed with her display of emotions, he abruptly got up and walked away from the table.

The voluptuous accountant entered the room and walked right past Luv-Luv and picked up what was put on the table moments ago.

"Luv-Luv pull yourself together. It comes with the job, and you know this," the accountant whispered and walked out with everything.

"Luv-Luv your bath water is ready. C'mon so we can purge your troubles," the Persian maid said leading the tearful Luv-Luv by the hand. The loss of Sweety was all business and was the price she had to pay in order to play.

EPILOGUE

Day broke away from night and the sunlight was shining down in the Noware Housing Projects. On the motherless son, at 6:33 in the morning it was silent outside like a graveyard. Safe to say the double homicide had it like a ghost town in the atmosphere. No one was out and about but him. The world was cold alone, and the isolated wind made his lonely condition a little bit colder. The nine-year-old moved in slow motion as he walked through the gangway and found himself a seat on the hard-concrete steps. He had opened up shop on the porch of the recently beaten, shot and incarcerated convict mother's home. He wore black steel toed boots, white heavily starched denim pants, and brand-new black leather coat for warmth. Small-Time feeling chilly, he pulled the white mink fur trimmed hood over his head, 336 hours had come and gone since Spanish Fly was turned into Swiss cheese and Popcorn caught three to the dome.

Being blind to what happened to all the players of the past. Like time, crime would never stop. Small-Time was the next successor to fall in line to shine. From the pulpit of game, an ordained hustler ministered to him. It was calling to get money. The few grand he had to unhand under the foxy circumstances didn't belong to the little guy anyway. He wasn't hurting for certain. Shoe box money in the back of the closet had Small-Time back by popular demand. Power and position always switched quick in the fast lane. He was moving up in the brutal business world and in two more days, he was turning double digits. He was learning from life and death on how to gain wealth. He was chillin', sitting there chilly, remembering a lesson Spanish Fly had taught him about the grind, flashed through his mind.

Everybody wants to be somebody until somebody smoke 'em in front of everybody. Lil' man, ya hear me man? See this stuff right here? Don't sell this stuff to be seen, sell this stuff to make your means of life better. I've been watching you. I see you ain't got nobody, but you got the hustle and trust me lil' fella that's all you need. Small-Time snorted and spit yellow slimy mucus on the dirt as he thought about what Popcorn had said and how he didn't do too much talking. He was all about *foxy business*.

"Damn look at y'all now," he said to himself, looking across the sidewalk, where flowers were placed on the blood-stained concrete.

He began to stare at the spray-painted mural on the project building wall from an old picture of Popcorn and Spanish Fly when they were teenagers, facing each other posing in a fight stance. He spoke the words written under the mural. "Watch who's close to you." The two infamous criminals would forever be remembered as project heroes. The tales of Popcorn and Spanish Fly would be legendary and Small-Time wanted it to be the same for him. He sat on the steps with his hands in his pockets for heat. Small-Time could see kids in his age group dressed for the weather wearing back packs, leaving their homes, hiking to the bus stop, waiting for the bus to pick them up and take them to school. He was imagining himself, standing there with those children when a customer walked up, bringing him back to his reality.

"What it do nephew? Let me get two," the customer said. Small-Time quickly filled his order.

"You cool? I'll be here all day. Same thing," Small-Time said, taking the money, and holding it to the sky making sure everything was legit.

He folded the paper currency and stuffed it in his pocket. The customer shook his hand and moved on. Small-Time went back to dreaming again. Small-Time was watching the kids at the bus stop, horse playing, laughing and boys play fighting exemplifying their dukes. He was approached by another customer trying to get right.

"You got something, to give ya boy, u-dig," the slow talking customer requested. Small-Time like before moved quickly making the hand-to-hand transaction.

"You Big-Time now. Watch yaself, everybody wants the throne. Just look at that picture of them on the wall," said the slow talking customer.

Then the slow talking customer pointed at Popcorn and Spanish Fly's mural on the building across the street and walked off. Small-Time listened to the wisdom the lost soul provided but went back to watching the kids smiling and laughing. They all were loading on the school bus. Once everyone was seated the red stop sign on the yellow bus went out and they drove off. That's when the kid named Leaf blew down on him from out of nowhere. Small-Time quickly stood up from the hard-concrete steps. He was wondering where Leaf had come from.

"Oh, say it ain't so. Look what the wind blew down," Small-Time said slick-like, still surprised at the unexpected visit.

"Ain't see you in a minute. I heard you out here getting dumb money, sir. Shid, look out for ya boy. It's fucked up out here my dude. Let me hold a few dollars," Leaf asked suggestively. But Small-Time sensed snake intentions in Leaf's eyes which was more like a threat.

"Awe that's what ya on? Um a few bucks, a few bucks ain't nothing. Leaf you know I got you, huh?" Small-Time said reaching in his coat pocket putting his hand around his gun.

The sound of a black cat knocked over a garbage can caught Small-Time off guard and he turned his head for a split second, when he looked back Leaf had the luck of the draw. Small-Time was staring at a gray and black compact 9mm pointed at his chest. Small-Time wasn't going at gunpoint. He still tried to pull his pistol but was forced to stop. Pop-Pop-Pop-Pop! Leaf pulled the trigger putting four hot ones in his chest. Small-Time's little body fell to the concrete steps. His eyes were wide opened looking across the street past Leaf at the huge mural of Popcorn and Spanish Fly. He was trying his best to hold on. Small-Time's hand was still holding on to the gun in his pocket. Bah! The gun exploded from within his coat, the bullet pierced through the black leather coat, flying at Leaf's head. The kid jumped back startled, he just missed being struck by Small-Time's attempt to get his lick back. But, before he split for good, Leaf ran back up and stood over Small-Time, who was now gasping for air. Leaf aimed the gun at his head.

"You niggas killed my daddy, mothafucka," Leaf said.

Pop-Pop-Pop! Leaf otherwise known through the juvenile penal system as #R-00815 had pulled the trigger once again, blowing Small-Time's underdeveloped brain on the concrete steps. Leaf looked at the mangled body and flew away getting out of the projects. He made sure there would be no overtime tonight for Small-Time. His time was over. He had punched the clock and his time was up. Leaf had put the kid in time out forever.

The sanctified convict's mother made sure it was safe before she opened her door to see the kid murdered on her doorsteps.

"Ahhh! Ahhh! Lawd, lawd, not this little baby!" she cried out to the heavens.

No man, woman or child would be spared in a conflict of interest.

The end

Shout out to all my phony people/That set in my face and volunteered them lies y'all hurt my heart and yeah I cried but on the inside no teary eyed but I'm still here yes here he lies and don't got no time to sit and hear these lies/that's why they play y'all songs and fast forward and when they hear mine they hit rewind/now it's time for me to clear my mind/smokin' dope outta bong it's hippy time/beat a grown niggas ass with my belt like 'SAH-DAH-TAY-TIPPY-TAH'. That's Pooty Tang do you get me now/ I'm too stand up for you to sit me down I'm on the run for attempt right now and any other beef is 6ft down I know the definition of the word hollow but this here bullet ain't no empty round/I got so many niggas changing up on me it like a bitch when they walk they switching now/I'm so sick of bullshitting 'round I might rob my mans if he don't kick me down/ rob his ass at the top of the stair case laugh in his face then kick him down/I swear to God I ain't shitting 'round/I'm so high you gotta climb and get me down/whip my dick and start pissing down 'EWW' till you hear that trickling sound/Pissing on all y'all bitches who get a kick out of kicking a nigga when he down/You gotta fight hard you wanna beat me Even Oprah couldn't win free rounds/ My life is precious and I'll kill you for it with Rasfusha bullets them big ol' rounds/My bullets like the host of a show when you come through they tell you sit on down/got some hollow heads that will make you dance I call 'em Boogie bullets now get on down/You don't know who you dealing with call 411/get some info now.

ABOUT THE AUTHOR

Tyress "Tiger Woodz" Cunningham

You want to know me?

Been in the streets ever since I was fourteen years old.

Been locked up in jail thirty-one times.

Been to prison two times.

Been in rehab two times.

Been in a mental institution two times.

Tried to commit suicide two times.

Been stabbed three different times.

Been shot and grazed myself in the ankle.

Been homeless.

Been a bum.

Been a panhandler.

Been a clown.

Been a send off.

Been laughed at.

Been manipulated.

Been cheated on.

So, when you see me trying to do better and trying to win this time, understand where I have been before you say something about me. And the city of Rockford can vouch for everything I just said, it ain't no secret.

Tyress Cunningam resides in Illinois and is working on his

second book, No Hope. Connect with Tyress on Facebook.com/ tigerwoodz and Instagram.com/tyresscunningham

QUESTIONS AND TOPICS FOR DISCUSSION

1. The author, Tyress Cunningham, has an amazing writing style, one that captivates the reader from the opening paragraphs. At the very beginning of the storyline, we are in the midst of a shootout between two friends, Spanish Fly and Popcorn, over a conflict of intere$t. As the plot thickens, what do you see is the real cause of their conflict of intere$t?

2. Are you team Popcorn or team Spanish Fly?

3. This is an urban fiction tale of how things can go wrong when jealously enters the picture. How realistic was the storyline to anything you may or may not have experienced in your own life?

4. We also witness a friendship between two women, Luv Luv and Sweety, how did their loyalty towards one another impact what happened between Spanish Fly and Popcorn?

5. The character Small-Time was an integral figure in the storyline. Were you surprised at the outcome of this character? Would you have wanted to see more regarding this character? Why or why not?

6. The character Macvicious was an interesting character, did any of his character traits affect you? How or how

not?

7. Out of all the characters in the book, who was your favorite character and why?

8. Why do you think Popcorn's Uncle Seville made the comment, "You ain't got no friends"?

9. Throughout all the drama, the characters, seemed to be 'businessmen' in their own right, what does this tell you about each one's goal in life and/or their individual fate.

10. The names of every character in the book seem to shed some insight to the personality of each character. In your opinion, who's name fit that character the most and why?

11. Most of what took place was in the city's projects, do you think the storyline's location was important to the events in the story? If so, why, or why not?

12. How would you describe this novella in one sentence to a friend?

www.ingramcontent.com/pod-product-compliance
Lightning Source LLC
Chambersburg PA
CBHW030743110726
47900CB00008B/2436